All That Dies in April

MARIANA TRAVACIO

All That Dies in April

Translated from the Spanish
by Will Morningstar & Samantha Schnee

WORLD EDITIONS
New York

Published in the USA in 2025 by World Editions NY LLC, New York

World Editions
New York

Copyright © Mariana Travacio, 2022

Original title *Quebrada*

First published in 2022 by Las afueras
English translation © Will Morningstar and Samantha Schnee, 2025
Cover image © "Nada de esto es un sueño. Arrieros en un camino."
Property of the Juan Rulfo Family.
Reproduction is prohibited without permission of the copyright holders.
Author portrait © Alejandro Jandry

Printed by Lightning Source, USA

This publication was made possible with the generous support
of the Fondation Jan Michalski.

Fondation
Jan Michalski

Library of Congress Cataloging in Publication Data is available

ISBN 978-1-64286-157-0

Company: worldeditions.org
Facebook: @WorldEditionsInternationalPublishing
Instagram: @WorldEdBooks
TikTok: @worldeditions_tok
Twitter: @WorldEdBooks
YouTube: World Editions

For Sonha Maria de França and,
in her name, for all kinds of dispossession,
for all the children we have watched walk away.

FIRST PART

And the sea lay in that wilderness
And my wilderness was nowhere

SOPHIA DE MELLO BREYNER

1

My name is Lina Ramos, wife of Relicario Cruz. For a while now I've been telling him we need to leave, but he doesn't want to. He's attached to this land, he says we were born here and we should die here, too. But we're the only ones left, I tell him. And he says we can't abandon our dead, we can't just go away and leave them behind, without anyone who knows them, Lina. That's what he says. That we can't do something like that. So I explain to him that I'd happily stay if there was enough food to eat. But we live in the quebrada, the land is good for nothing. The only things that grow here are pitiful weeds covered in thorns that claw at the wind. Everything else is rock, stone. And it takes forever to get around because it's so steep; nothing but sharp, sheer cliffs. The other day I was feeling unwell so I had to go see Octavia, who knows how to make me feel better. I spent four hours clambering over rocks. When I got there I was on my last legs. I tell Relicario all of this, but he doesn't listen to me. He says that we can't abandon this place. That if we leave, the dead will become nameless and confused, because no one will be left to remind them who they were or what they said or what they liked. And you just don't do that, Lina. We must stay to visit them, bring them a sip of rum and some soup, or whatever they had when they were alive. That's what he says: if we leave, who's going to bring them their rum, who's going to remind them about things; we can't go, Lina. So I try to explain that no one wants to abandon anyone, but he should try to think about us a little, too, because there's no future here. This land provides nothing, Cruz, less and less each day, it hardly even rains here anymore. Sometimes a couple of clouds appear and we stare at them like they might bring us some water but the quebrada rejects them and they go somewhere else to rain. That's what I tell him. But he's hardheaded and doesn't want to take any chances: he wants to stay, period, and then he asks me, where would we live, Lina, we're getting too old. And I don't know how to reply, because I've spent my whole life among these rocks and what can I say if I don't know anything about the wider world. Don't say anything, Lina, I tell myself when I see my entreaties fall on deaf ears. The only thing that makes me feel better is thinking that tomorrow I'll try again. Then tomorrow comes and I raise my eyes to the empty sky and feel a weariness eating away at me inside. So I gather my courage and insist: let's go, Relicario. The moment I awaken I see the cloudless sky with no birds, completely empty, nothing new under the sun. The sky always looks the same and it makes me feel so empty, too. I've been saying the same thing for fourteen years now, but he doesn't hear me. Fourteen years, since my brother left with our son, our Tala, who I miss so much. Sometimes I get so tired of repeating myself that I lose my will to go on. But if I don't keep on insisting, death will come find us all shriveled up next to our dead, and there will be no one left to bring us some rum or soup or anything else. Some days I feel like he might actually hear what I'm saying. Some days I say my prayers to the holy lord, but he doesn't hear me either. He must have gone deaf, I think. I'm a faithful believer, and Relicario is, too. But lately I've had it in for God because he hasn't answered a single one of my prayers. And sometimes I just get furious. Anger that lasts for days. Whenever it happens I tell Cruz that the good lord must be deaf, or maybe he's abandoned this place, too; even he must get tired of all this rock. And when I come to him with these ideas, Cruz says I should stop making things up. That God is everywhere. And I tell him that he may be everywhere, but he's not here because it's too hard to get to. We're hemmed in here, Cruz, in this quebrada. You have to look up high, so high, just to see the sky. But he doesn't like hearing these things. He huffs at me and retreats to his workshop, which makes me so mad that I get sick and have to go see Octavia to get better. It's a shame she lives so far away. Depending on the wind, it takes four hours to get to where she lives, sometimes five or more. But she's the only one who knows how to make me better, so I go anyway. At first I move quickly, even though it's uphill, but then the trail falls away. From there you have to find your own way, clambering over rocks. It takes a really long time and it's exhausting, but I approach it with determination. As soon as I arrive Octavia appears, as if she's been waiting for me. Sometimes she emerges from inside; other times I see her coming from behind the hut, where she grows the herbs she uses for her remedies. And I feel calmer just seeing her. She immediately brings me inside and makes me some kind of concoction before I even tell her anything, and soon I feel better so we start to talk. In the beginning I didn't talk to her much. I hardly said anything, I just thanked her for her efforts. But these days I tell her a lot. I tell her how tired I am of begging Relicario, how he doesn't seem to hear me, how he doesn't give me the slightest hope that we'll ever leave this place. I'm getting old, Octavia, and I don't know what to do. Sometimes I think Relicario's right, we shouldn't abandon the dead, but my longing to leave has grown so strong that it keeps me awake at night. Night comes and even Christ cannot help me. My eyes stay open, exposed, sleepless. And when it starts to get light and I leave our house to fetch water to brew the maté, exhaustion creeps up my back and leaves me all hunched over like this. I need to sleep, Octavia, so I can stand straight again.

2

I'm leaving, Relicario.

Where do you think you're going to go all alone, Lina?

Octavia told me which way to go.

What way, Lina, there's no way out of here.

You have to go straight down until you get to the stream.

What stream, Lina, be serious.

That's what Octavia told me. To keep going down, all the way to the stream. And to look carefully at which way the water's flowing and keep going, following the water. That the water goes to the river and the river goes to the sea. Let's go to the sea, Cruz. Let's go together.

You're crazy, Lina. Even if there was a stream it would have dried up years ago.

3

She took our two big canteens and a bundle of clothes and the fistful of seeds Octavia had given her for the journey. These are good seeds, Octavia had told her, they'll give you strength. Use them when you need them. Stubborn as a mule, my Lina, leaving to go look for that stream. We argued on her last night. I didn't want her to go and she didn't want to go alone: she wanted to drag me along with her. She was adamant. Come on, Cruz, let's go find the sea. Over and over. But I didn't want any part of this trouble that had grown inside her. You can't just do something like this, Lina. But she didn't hear me. Headstrong, she was. And now God knows where she is. It's been more than a week since she left. I was sure she'd come right back. That's what I told her as she was walking out the door. Don't be stubborn, Lina, enough of this madness. What's the point. You're just going to come right back. You'll see, in two or three days you'll be right back here. Do you really think you'll be able to get anywhere on your own. You've never been anywhere else but here. But it was no use. No matter how hard I tried, she was stuck on this idea of going to the sea. And now I wake up every morning so angry I start to shake. You can't just abandon your husband, your land, your dead. You can't abandon them, Lina. What kind of woman does that. We're too old to go trying our luck out there in the world. But I should have known long ago, before I married her: Lina was a Ramos. And you could never talk a Ramos out of anything. No wonder that brother of hers was the way he was, coming and taking El Tala and leaving us here, with no son and no help.

4

She told me to keep going down, down, down. That's what I'm doing. But I've been going down for three days and there's no stream. Maybe I should have stayed. Octavia said three days, give or take. Two if I made good time. But I can't go any faster because the descent is steep and getting steeper, and it has so many twists and turns that I can't see ahead. I have to take small steps and be careful where I put my feet. Every step scares me. All these jagged rocks. I wonder if this place will eventually become flat. I want to walk on level ground, see some grass, anything that grows from the earth. I'll keep going down, Octavia, but I don't see the stream and I don't have much water left. I'll keep going as long as there's daylight. There's probably not much left. Maybe two hours until the sun sets. I don't like walking at night. Even though there are so many stars, they don't give much light, at least not enough to see. The moon has been waning; I can't proceed without the sun. Now it's at my back, coming from the quebrada, stretching my body along the path. It looks like the body of a rag doll being jerked along the bleached rocks. Yet my shadow is more agile than these old bones. At this time of day it's not so hot. If I hurry, who knows, maybe I'll find the stream before dark. I'll keep walking until the last ray of light. If it's really three days,

I might see the stream tonight and see which way the water's flowing and find some grass where I can rest my bones. The rocks are hard, they don't make it easy to rest. I've been sleeping like that the last two nights, unable to find a place where the rocks don't dig into me. The only good thing about them is they preserve the heat. When night falls and the air cools, the rocks remain warm. Providing a kind of shelter. They keep your legs warm and you lie still while the stars in the sky complete their rotation up above.

5

He was thirteen, El Tala, when Camilo showed up talking about the rainforest. He said there was work, with all the wood. That we had less than nothing here. That we should let him go. That he'd take El Tala too, so he could fulfill his destiny. He really said that: I'll take him so he can fulfill his destiny. And Lina agreed. She had a weakness for him, her younger brother. She trusted him. Then fourteen years went by and we never heard another word. Not about Camilo, not about our son. Sometimes I think about the forest. Camilo told us there were rivers and plenty of rain to make things grow. He said that was why there were so many trees and so much work, with all the wood. And they must have all kinds of animals we don't have, because nothing grows here and we hardly have any animals. She's right about that, Lina is. There's nothing here. Except these rocky spikes that spring up from the earth and the guinea pigs that race by as if the devil himself were chasing them and the few goats that graze for whatever they can find among these dried-out weeds. But our dead are here. And I was taught you don't leave your dead behind. None of that mattered to her, to Lina. She let Camilo take our Tala and then she left too. I'm the only one who hasn't left. But I don't want to. I know there's no future here but I also know that in other places the present doesn't have much going for it either. So stubborn, Lina. She shouldn't have gone. It's been two weeks now. I thought she'd be back already. She must have found the stream, the one Octavia told her about. If she hadn't, she'd be back by now. Or maybe she got lost. Who knows.

6

Octavia's words nagged at me with the persistence of a hungry dog. Three days, she said. I started to worry I had lost track of time. But I hadn't. It was surely the third day if I had slept under the stars for two nights running. So I forced myself to keep going: a little farther, Lina, a little farther. But the night was getting on. There wasn't any light in the sky to help me. If the moon was up, it was somewhere else. There were only stars, weak ones. There were a lot of them and they glimmered faintly, but they couldn't help me see. It must have been late, because the wind was blowing cold and making it hard to continue. So I settled down out of the wind and went to sleep. I must have been exhausted because the next morning I didn't awaken at dawn, only much later when the sun was high. I felt a bit dizzy, maybe from sleeping so much. I felt a pang of regret and thought of Cruz asking me not to go, asking me to stay, telling me you can't do things like that. I started to answer him out loud, as if he could hear me. Walking down the slope and talking to myself. I've waited too long for you, Cruz, and now I've come too far to return. I'm going to find that stream. At times I felt like the mountain was endless, that I could continue descending it until I reached hell itself. And that's what I was thinking when I spotted some goats far below. Where it was really steep. It wasn't easy to get there; the slope seemed to fall straight down from the sky. But it gave me hope to see those animals, so I kept going. And as I was approaching them two women appeared. They came over quickly, as soon as they heard me. And I must have looked at them with desperation in my eyes because they immediately asked if I needed anything. Where's the stream, I asked. They pointed downward: just over there, señora, about half an hour at a good pace. We're going there now, as soon as our friend arrives; if you're not in a hurry, you can come with us. And when I heard this, I immediately accepted their offer. I was tired of walking alone. They invited me to sit with them on some stones. They seemed like mother and daughter. One looked more worn-out than the other. The younger one offered me some milk. I accepted and tried to take small sips; I didn't want them to notice how hungry I was.

7

I made a decision, mother. You taught me not to abandon the dead, and I understand. But the house is unbearable since my Lina left and I'm not the kind of man to live alone. I can't get used to it. This land never seemed so bad before, back when her leaving was all talk. But now that she's gone and isn't coming back, I've started waking up every morning sick with resentment. Don't take it the wrong way, mother. I know how close you feel to this land but you have to understand that even the little rain we used to get doesn't come anymore. But I won't leave you here alone, don't worry. That's why I went to speak with Don Amancio the other day. Do you remember Amancio, mother? Exactly, the one who lives down the way and sells rum. His daughter got married and I heard they were looking for a house. So I had an idea. I went to see him and we talked for a long time, past nightfall. I didn't know how best to tell him. I'd gotten to his place in the early afternoon, with the sun still raging. He offered me a little cold water and some rum and we got to talking. First I asked about his daughter. He told me she'd gotten pregnant and that was why they were looking for a house. I pretended not to know already. So I started to tell him. I said Lina had gone away and I was unhappy without her, alone in the house. I made him an offer: I'd give him the house to give to his daughter if he got me what I needed so I could leave. It took us a while to come to an agreement, because you'll remember that Amancio has a bit of a tight fist. He doesn't like to let go of things. And he's shrewd. But I didn't have anywhere else to be. So I listened to his reasoning and gave him my own. I made it clear that he could have the house with everything in it. His daughter wouldn't need to get anything. Not a table, not even a knife. We closed the deal with some rum as the stars came into view through the half-open door.

He said he'd need a few days to get everything together. That's why I came to see you today, mother. In a few days, you're coming with me. And don't get mad, because father's coming too. The only thing I can't do, mother, is take all the rest of your dead. I'm sorry, but Amancio said he could only get me one donkey. I asked him for two donkeys and a good wagon. But he said he couldn't get two donkeys, so I'd have to make do with the one. And you know that we can't go overburdening the animal, mother, because the land is steep. And that the only wagons around here are narrow ones, seeing as there aren't any paths wide enough to pull anything too big. So you'll have to forgive me, but I'm taking you two and no one else.

8

It was a long time before their friend showed up. I started to get antsy, but I didn't want to say anything. I stayed quiet, suppressing my urge to ask them why she was taking so long. They didn't seem to be in any rush. They told me that they came down every day for the goats to get some water. It wasn't far. Each day they came down with their goats and returned. The years must have added up for them like they had for me, staring at the same sky, but now I had places to go. Still, I decided to wait. When I got to the stream I would see which way it flowed and know which direction to take. I was in no hurry either. The idea of seeing that stream, knowing that Octavia had been right, calmed me.

The friend they were waiting for turned out to be a young woman. She showed up late with her goat, in no hurry at all. Her name was Hermelinda, they said. That's how they introduced her when she arrived. She was so beautiful you couldn't look at her: she looked like she was from another world. God must have been overjoyed to create such a creature. I had never seen such beauty. Her black eyes had a strength that left me speechless. And her hair fell like a waterfall to her waist. It was hard not to stare at her. But I acted like I was thinking about something else and the four of us climbed down to the stream together. When I saw it,

I was a little taken aback. Is that thing down there the stream, I asked. Of course, they replied. Where's the water, it looks empty. That's the stream, they said. When we got closer I could see it better: it was a trickle of water running between the stones. That's not much water, I told them. Well that's the stream, doña. That's all that's left. There used to be more, but that's all there is now. They seemed unbothered by it, those women and their goats. I didn't want to offend them so I didn't say anything. I couldn't take my eyes off that sad excuse for a stream. I was trying to figure out which way the water was flowing, but it didn't seem to be going anywhere. It didn't have enough strength to flow, I thought, but still I stared at it. It had to be going somewhere. What are you looking at, doña, they asked me. I was ashamed to tell them. So I said it was just nice to see the water, and I scooped some up to drink. I liked drinking from the stream. The water was cool and I was thirsty. Then the women said that it was time for them to go and I felt both relieved and sad. Suddenly I was alone again, not knowing which direction to take, but it was a relief not to have them asking me questions. They were already moving up the mountain when Hermelinda turned around: where are you going, she asked me. I didn't have a chance to reply because the others told her that I was going to the sea. I just nodded.

9

Please, mother, I'm asking you to understand. Forgive me for speaking to you like this, I mean no disrespect. But the fact is without Lina I can't go on. You can come with me if you want. But your parents will have to wait. There's no way to bring them along right now. We can come back to get them later, after we find Lina. You never know, maybe we'll find her soon and we can all come right back here. But in the meantime, please don't ask me for that, mother. There's just no way to bring all of your dead. I can barely manage you and father. I'm sorry, but I can't climb all over the quebrada with so much company. Remember, Lina has a month's head start and we have to catch up with her somehow. I'm going to see Doña Octavia before we leave. I want to ask her what she told Lina so we can be sure to go in a good direction. We'll have to feel our way along no matter what, with the paths around here being as devious as they are, and who knows if Lina even followed Octavia's advice. We just have to keep faith that we'll find her. She was on foot, but we'll have a wagon. Not that the donkey will be much help, but at least we won't get as tired. With Octavia's directions, maybe we'll pick up her trail. Amancio still has to let me know how he's made out. I asked for a few things so we'll see if he can get his hands on them. I offered him everything I have in exchange. At the time, it seemed like a fair trade. I hope Lina doesn't get angry with me, leaving her without a house. I just couldn't see any other way. To be honest, she wasn't entirely wrong, Lina. Things have gotten pretty bad here. The land looks so empty these days. Anyone with any life left in them has already gone away to try their luck somewhere else. It's just us old folks here now, watching each day come and go, same as the last. If you could see it, mother, it would make you cry. It's just us and the mountains, in this land without water. Not even the weeds grow like they used to. They're already dry by the time they come up, and they give out before the first leaf even has a chance. The only thing they offer us are thorns, so tough that even the wind complains when it passes by.

They'd been quite talkative, those women. While we were waiting for their friend, they wanted to know where I was from and where I was going. I didn't want to tell them much. I just said I wanted to see the sea. As soon as I opened my mouth I regretted it: I was afraid they'd think I was crazy. But they didn't say anything; after a while the older one asked me where it was. So I told them what Octavia had said: follow the stream all the way to the river, and the river should lead me to the sea. You have to go where the water's going, that's what I told them. They listened to me carefully. Then they began speaking to each other, so I got off the rock I was sitting on and took a few steps away from them. They were talking about another land, a place where there was plenty of grass and rain and work. I gathered that they were hoping their friend would find a job there, because there was an opportunity and she was young enough to go and try her luck in that land. I moved closer to them and they told me: look, in that place there's fertile land; not like this wretched land of ours. They stood up to show me where it was, pointing to the mountains facing us. You couldn't see anything beyond their peaks, yet they insisted, pointing their fingers: over there, on the other side of the mountains, there are hills. That place is on the other side of those hills. We've been told the land is good there, doña, and there's water and there's work. It was hard for me to imagine what a place like that would look like, but they sure seemed excited about it.

Octavia wasn't surprised when I showed up at her house. She came out calmly from inside to welcome me. What can I do for you, friend. I came to see you, doña, because my Lina left me and the days have been hard. The house is lonely now: it's been fourteen years without El Tala, and now my wife is gone, too. When she left she said she was going to the sea. And I've decided to go and look for her. Don Amancio is finding me a wagon and a donkey, so I'll be leaving soon. I'm bringing my people. That's why I had to ask him, Don Amancio, for the wagon. But before I go, I had to come ask you if you know where I can find her.

Doña Octavia was silent for a moment, as if she were searching for the words. After a while, she spoke: what you are asking me to do is not easy. It's true I told Lina where to go, but I can't tell you where she went. All I can tell you is which path I told her to take, but that won't be enough to track her down. There's no way to give you the certainty you seek: you must not forget that the path will unfold only once the journey begins.

And that was all Octavia said. It was four hours there and four hours back just for that old witch to tell me absolutely nothing. I thanked her anyway, because I have my manners, but I climbed down from her house cursing every single twinkling star in the sky that night. And I was still cursing when I curled up on my cot to rest my bones.

12

Deep down, I was relieved that the women with the goats had left: it meant I could carry on my way without having to explain where I was going. I was reassured to be there, by the stream, because Octavia had been right: there really was a stream. And if there was a stream, that meant there was a river. Which cheered me up a lot. Enough to keep on going, but the day was getting on. The sky began to darken. I thought it would be a good idea to stay there and sleep by the water. I was happy that though the wind had continued to blow up above it hadn't bothered to come down the mountain and trouble me. When the sky turned black I stopped looking at the water, which seemed to be singing to me. I fell asleep to its song that night.

Tomorrow, Amancio told me. That's why I came to see you, father. Because there isn't much time left. Mother says she wants me to bring her parents, but just imagine me trying to find Lina when I'm dragging so many people around with me. I can't, father. I know you don't worry as much and you wouldn't go asking for things like that, but you know her, you know mother: she's relentless. She doesn't want to hear a word about leaving without her people. And it's no good explaining that there are too many of them because she already told me she doesn't just want to bring her parents. She wants to bring her brothers and sisters and her grandfather, too. Imagine, father, if I tried to take everyone. You remember what the paths around here are like, barely wide enough for a narrow wagon to squeeze by. I should be traveling light, without the wagon, without anything. But that's the way it is and I'm bringing you both, call me stubborn. I don't want to leave you all alone. Oh, father, if only you could change her mind. I know, you don't have to tell me twice: you could never change her mind about anything. You always stood by her. Anyway, father, that's where we are. We'll have to leave soon. I went to Amancio's today, after recovering from that useless visit to Doña Octavia. The old witch was no help at all. She just told me which way she'd told Lina to go, but then she said that wasn't enough. And of course it wasn't, because how can we know where Lina actually went, not to mention what she might have run into along the way. I didn't go all the way to see that witch for her to tell me something anyone could have figured out on their own. I went so she'd give me something to be sure about. But I've got nothing. All I'm sure of now, father, is that we will leave this place very soon. And it's hard, because while this land isn't much, we were born here. We are who we are here. If we leave we'll have to keep explaining where we're from and where we're going. And that doesn't sound very appealing to me. But like I told mother, it's not like we have a whole lot to keep us going here. Lina had been telling me for a while but I wasn't much for listening. I'm still not even sure if I really agree. Because it all depends, father. On the one hand, it's true that this place has seen better days. On the other, it's no small thing to abandon your home when you have no idea what's waiting for you out there. I always liked the calm of our little house, each day the same, with my Lina. There was a certain kind of peace, I can't explain it, even though El Tala wasn't with us. But I think we got used to passing the days alone, anyway. Or I did, at least. Because Lina was never the same after her brother left with El Tala. She started to resent this land. She complained that it never gave us anything and we should go find a better life. I think Lina ended up leaving out of regret, for having let her brother take El Tala away. It was too late by the time she started having second thoughts. They'd left without knowing where they were going, so there was no way she could have found them. Wherever they ended up, things must have turned out well, because they never came back. Or else they died on the way, God only knows. We wondered more than once about where that rainforest might be. There were so many times we thought about going to find them, but we didn't have a clue about where they could have gone. That's why now is the time for me to go and find my Lina. I think it's still early enough, and I have an idea of which way she might have gone. We can't be completely sure, father, but I want to try. See if you can talk to mother and explain that the wagon will only fit the two of you.

14

The sound of the water hitting the rocks awoke me. I don't know what had happened to the stream but when the sun came up it was so full of water that I had to rub my eyes to make sure I was seeing straight. I decided that it must have rained a lot up in the sky or somewhere else in the world for so much water to be rushing past. When I looked at it I had no doubt: I knew exactly which direction the stream was going. It made me so happy that I looked to the heavens and thanked the good lord and I even wished I could tell Cruz that God did exist in this part of the world: if you had only come with me, Cruz, God is here. It's not like you said, that he's everywhere. He's not up there in the quebrada, of that I'm certain. But he really is here: this stream was dry yesterday and today it's full. I should have known because I heard its song while I slept. But I never imagined that the song was all this water that had started to flow by. I wish you could be here, Relicario, to see all this water.

I tried to look up ahead, in the direction the stream was flowing: I was curious about the road that lay before me. But it was too twisty: the stream was so serpentine it was impossible to see. And I was so intrigued that I picked up my bundle of clothes and began following the water. Now, I had no idea how many days it would take to get to the river, but at least

I didn't have to worry about where I was stepping. All I had to do was walk alongside it. And my feet seemed to move more quickly on those banks.

15

Don Amancio came by with his daughter. He told me they would be coming: to please forgive him, but his daughter wanted to get acquainted with the place, if I didn't mind. It's no problem, I told him. And so they came, the two of them, to get acquainted. As it happened, Don Amancio had already been to the house once. But that was a long time ago. El Tala must have been a year old when he was struck with that fever, the one that left him shaking all through the night. We didn't know what to do. I went down to the village, desperate for help. And it was Don Amancio who volunteered that night. He came with his family's healer, may he rest in peace. A good man. He saved the boy, he saved El Tala, and I never forgot that day. And since then I've had a lot of respect for Don Amancio; he might be tightfisted with his things, but he was generous toward us. How could I mind if his daughter wanted to come and get acquainted with our house. It did make me a little embarrassed, their visit, because I didn't have much to show them. The girl came inside with an eager look in her eyes. Amancio gave her permission. And when she was done, she thanked her father and thanked me too, for the visit, and right then and there Amancio told me he could deliver what I'd asked for the next day. And I don't know where I got the nerve but I asked him to give me just a few more days, to wrap up my affairs. He looked at his daughter and then turned to me with those gray eyebrows of his and asked if three days were enough for me to wrap everything up, to say goodbye.

No one had told me it would be such a long time before I saw another soul on my journey. After the women with the goats, I didn't cross paths with anyone for ages. My legs were beginning to grow weak when I saw the dogs. They were drinking thirstily. There were two goatherds with them, and lots of goats, and some women who were filling jugs with water. I was so happy to see them. They must have noticed my excitement because the women came over right away to ask if they could help me. I didn't know what to say. I told them I had been walking for some time without seeing anyone. They asked me if I was lost. I explained that I wasn't exactly lost, it was just that my journey was so long. That I was looking for a river, and was it still far away. They looked at me, puzzled. They called the goatherds over and suddenly everyone was asking where the river was. None of them seemed to recall a river anywhere nearby. They pointed in one direction and then another, they couldn't agree. In the end, their verdict: no, doña, there's no river here. And when I heard that, all my joints gave way. I felt myself fall to the ground like a rag doll. They said they spent quite a while trying to revive me, until they decided to take me to one of their homes. I awoke in a strange house. It belonged to a couple. I must have been in their way. I was so embarrassed when I learned what had happened. Several of them had carried me to the cot where I was lying and went to get help. A friend who knew about such things came to see me and told them my stomach was empty. They let me eat and drink for some time. They even offered to let me stay with them until I felt strong enough to continue my journey. And my shame grew as I realized how much trouble I was causing them. So I told them I didn't want to be a bother, not to worry about me, I'd be fine. But they kept on insisting until I agreed to stay. The lady of the house began speaking to me in her soft voice, like she was singing a lullaby. Her name was Balbina. It was a joy to listen to her and I liked that she didn't ask me questions. She just gave me advice. That I needed to build my strength before continuing on my journey. That if I didn't, I wouldn't make it to my river or anywhere else. And that if I wasn't sure where I was going I shouldn't wander around aimlessly; I should prepare myself. That she had heard from her husband's mouth there was a place where I could find work. That maybe I should stop and work a little while before I continued my journey. And I paid careful attention to her, because what she said made sense to me. And then I told her about the women with the goats, who had already told me about the place where grass was plentiful. But I had come away with the idea that this place was very far away. I wondered how I would find it without getting lost. I imagined myself walking endlessly, aimlessly. So I'd decided to follow the stream. Because I knew it would take me to the river. And the river goes to the sea, I said, and I want to see the sea. And while I said this she looked at me admiringly, with no disapproval. So much that the next day she came and told me that she had told her husband about my situation. And that they were considering how they could help me. And she confessed that I reminded her of her mother, which is why she wanted to lend me a hand, because of my similarities with her mother: that my eyes had the same spark. That's what she said. And I was deeply moved when I heard her tell me this. And so her husband went to talk to a friend who knew the region well. They did so much for me, I don't know how I'll ever be able to repay them. In the end, it seems that this friend might be able to take me. He says he'll let me know tomorrow whether or not he can bring me with him, so I can find work. And if there's no job for me, I'll return. That night it was hard to fall asleep, but it wasn't a sleepless night like the kind I'd had before. It wasn't due to my resentment at seeing the same sky day after day. Now I was in a strange house and tomorrow was full of promise.

I'd been warned that it wouldn't be easy to go digging up the dead. I had some new coffins with me, because I'd also been warned the old coffins would be in pieces by now. It was a good thing I'd remembered to ask Don Amancio for the new ones. And it was a good thing I remembered to ask him for a sturdy shovel too. I got there early because there's not much a person can do when the sun is beating down on them. It was still night when I arrived, but it wasn't so cold under that moonless sky. The moon doesn't show its face much around here. It was almost like working with my eyes closed at the start, by the meager light of the stars, but I knew the sun would be up soon and then I'd be able to see better. Meanwhile, there I was with the shovel, next to my mother's grave. I didn't want to go rooting around in someone else's space so I was careful to find the right spot. That set me back longer than I thought it would, but I was still feeling hopeful. I had the wagon Don Amancio had gotten me. And Jumento, my new donkey. And having them felt almost like sanctuary. It's true there was no light, no moon, just our same old barren sky, but I had the wagon and I had my donkey and on top of that I had a good shovel and the two shiny coffins I'd asked for. That was enough for me. I didn't care anymore about what my mother or her dead had to say. The rest of them would just have to stay put and wait. All I could think about now was leaving to look for my Lina, just me and my things. I wasn't even upset about giving up the house anymore. The point is, it was still dark as I went over to my mother and father's graves, when I told them it was time for us to go. But the first shovelfuls tested all my resolve. I was alone. The dark sky winked with what little light it had to offer. I'd have to settle for that. Your eyes get used to it after a while, anyway. Digging up mother took more than two hours. I talked to her the whole time, gently, so she wouldn't get angry. I told her: I'm sorry to come and disturb you like this, mother, but tomorrow we're leaving and I have no choice but to get you out now. And so I kept talking and digging and as the sky started to brighten I could see there was no coffin left. The earth had devoured it. My mother was nothing but bones in a hole in the ground. I took her out bone by bone, carefully putting her in her new coffin. Then I fastened the coffin with rope and heaved her up onto the wagon. By the time I finished with mother, I didn't think I had it in me to dig up father. I looked at my donkey: I don't have it in me, I confessed. Not for digging up father, not for going anywhere at all. But there was no turning back, seeing as I'd already promised the house to Don Amancio. The whole thing started to seem like a terrible idea. I don't know how the hell I got myself mixed up in all this mess. My donkey looked at me with those enormous eyes of his and didn't say a word. I heaved a sigh, slung my shovel over my shoulder, and got to work on the next grave.

18

They told me the goatherd's name was Feliciano. That he was leaving early the next morning. That he could take me with him if I liked. That he and his donkey knew the road well because they went there every year for work. It was far away, that place. We'd be on the road for at least two weeks just crossing the mountains. If I wanted I could go with him the next morning. They had made him promise to stop by before he left. That's what Balbina and her husband told me that night. And I clasped Balbina's hands and looked deep into her sad eyes: I would never forget her and all the help she had given me. And a tear rolled down my cheek, and I looked at her husband and thanked him as well, and then I thanked the holy lord, and then I remembered Octavia and thanked her, too, and I think I fell asleep and continued to thank everyone in my dreams.

I took father out bone by bone too. He was the same as mother, the coffin rotted away. They must have been pleased, those two, to have gone one after the other like they did. There had always been such pride in their eyes when they looked at each other. That was the one thing they never lacked. Every day, they fell asleep and woke up at the same time, as if they were a single person. And seeing each other again each morning gave them so much joy. The days could have been of feast or famine, it didn't matter. Just opening their eyes and finding themselves still together seemed to be enough. Father's eyes started to fade as soon as mother got sick. And when mother died and father came back from the burial, he went to sleep and never woke up. We buried him the next day, in the grave beside hers. It was a comfort to know they could sleep side by side down in the earth too. And now I had them with me, on this narrow wagon. They only just fit, one on top of the other. It was a relief, knowing I could take them with me, together.

Don Amancio and his daughter came to see me off. They helped load my things onto the wagon, around the coffins. Not long after setting out, I turned back to look at the house. Amancio was still standing there, next to the door. He raised his hat. I responded in kind. Then I looked at the way ahead and said to my donkey: come on, Jumento, let's go find Lina.

20

Feliciano's skin was weathered by the elements. You could tell he was a goatherd. My brother told me that goatherds are good at conversation. That the job is an excuse to talk to yourself. They go around talking to themselves all day, he said. They say one thing and then they reply. Then they say the opposite and reply again. That's how they are. Camilo enjoyed the company of every goatherd he crossed paths with. He'd start a conversation just to hear them say something and then, a little while later, state the contrary with the same conviction, like they were two people in one. And when I remembered what Camilo had said I began to feel comfortable with this Feliciano. As I said: his skin was weathered, and he had a good sense of direction. He must have spent many hours wandering through the region. The donkey knew the road well, he said: donkeys have good memories. And I listened to him while I thought of my brother and we walked calmly along, side by side with the donkey. It had long eyelashes and always watched the ground and never complained. He was very courteous with me, that Feliciano. He said it wouldn't be right for him to ride the donkey. He had only one and he wasn't going to make a lady walk. That's how he put it: that we would both walk together. The donkey would carry our things. And not to worry, there were enough provisions for us to reach our destination without going hungry. The donkey guided us and I relaxed alongside it. It was a different way of traveling. I didn't have to worry about which direction I should go or getting lost. At some point I asked him what the land was like where we were going. He took a moment to reply. Listen, señora, he said, you won't believe your eyes when we get there. It's a land of plenty. I have no doubts you've never seen anything like it. It's not just that it rains, which in itself is remarkable, it's that everything there is too much. You'll see. That land produces everything in abundance. It's strange. When it rains, it rains a lot. Sometimes it rains for a whole month without stopping for a second. The people get tired of so much rain falling from the sky. It happens sometimes. And when it rains like that, day after day, it's a constant rain. Like steady weeping. At other times the rain gets violent. When it rains violently, the sky fills with lightning. You'll see, señora. Those flashes furrow the sky and they're followed by a sound that's deafening. That's how it is when it storms. Especially at night. It's like God is displeased and unleashes all these angry things in the sky. When that happens, it's good to have a place to take shelter. You'll see those skies. And you'll see those clouds. Sometimes they come so low that you're walking inside them. It's like they're made of smoke. And sometimes they're so high up in the sky that they seem very far away. And sometimes they're gray and they're heavy with water. And sometimes they extend so far that they look like one enormous cloud that covers everything. And sometimes they appear broken, like the wind has torn them to bits and left them hanging there in the sky. And, like I was saying, that's what the sky and the days and the people are like there. It's a place of excess. Everything proliferates there, señora. You'll see all this abundance for yourself when we arrive.

And as I listened to Feliciano, I didn't want him to stop. I asked him to keep telling me more. And that's when he told me not to get too excited: don't get too excited, doña, that would be a mistake. When I say too much of everything, what I mean is: it's all too much. Because there's a lot of madness there, too, doña. You'll soon see it with your own eyes.

Once I was on my way, with my parents and my donkey, the future seemed out of my hands. I stopped wondering whether I was doing the right thing or the wrong thing. I stopped thinking about the house and everything I had left behind. I stopped asking myself whether Lina would have been annoyed with me for trading our house for a wagon and a donkey. I just thought about how I missed Lina, even though she was stubborn and we'd never seen eye to eye on everything the way my parents had. She was willful, Lina was, pigheaded. But it didn't make sense anymore to take her to task for it. I'm on my way. I'll search for that stream, Lina. And when I find the stream, I'll follow it to the river. And when I make it to the river, I'll go in search of the sea, until I find you.

The first night we slept beneath a sky shot full of stars. That day had seemed like it would never end: we had left at dawn and carried on walking even after night had fallen. Feliciano told me that it would be good to go a little farther that first day, if I was able, so we could make it to the first mountain the next day, which meant we'd make it to the stream on the other side of the mountain, and that was where we'd get our water and the donkey's. I told him yes, he could count on me, I would keep going as long as necessary. I felt safe and I was captivated by his stories, and I was eager to get to that land as soon as I could. I felt like I would never tire.

The night was our generous blanket, neither cold nor windy. We awoke at the first light of day. Feliciano watered his donkey and offered me a little too. I was thirsty but I drank carefully because I knew that water had to last until we had made it over the mountain.

As soon as we were awake Feliciano said: today is all uphill. If you get tired, he said, we'll take a break. I listened to him carefully, looking at him with thanks. I was so eager to get there I couldn't have cared less whether it was uphill or downhill. I told him it was no problem, I would walk as far as he wanted. So we started going uphill that morning in silence: he told me it would be better not to speak too much so we wouldn't lose our breath. And that we could speak in the evening if we liked. But as he had predicted, when we arrived that night we were so tired that we went to sleep without speaking or eating or anything else, we just wanted to rest our bones.

23

Jumento, I said to him that afternoon, what are we going to do about this hill. I looked down. There I was with my wagon and no idea how we were going to manage the descent. My donkey looked at me with his worried eyes. I tried to calm his nerves, to let him know I agreed with his assessment: no, I assured him, there's no way you're going down here. I remembered my father, who always said the best thing you could do with a donkey was to leave it alone, that they always find their own way. So that's what I told him: don't worry, we'll go whichever way you say. And Jumento looked at me with those big eyes of his, as if he understood. He went around to the other side, as if he'd decided to go back the way we'd come. So I told him to just keep in mind that we'd soon be needing water from the stream. Mother, I don't know whether he understood me or not. But I said it anyway, because all of a sudden we'd found ourselves on a cliff and there wasn't a hope in heaven that the donkey or any of the rest of us would be able to go down that way. So I let him back up like he wanted, so he could take us some other way. And the donkey just made a big circle, which took a good long while, the whole afternoon. By nightfall we were still near the cliff, but now a path forward had materialized. I kissed him on the head, my donkey, to show my gratitude for his skill. And then I gave him some food from the supply Don Amancio had given me as we were leaving. This is what the donkey eats, he'd told me, as he loaded the bale of hay onto the wagon with my things. So that was how we slept, that night, beside the wagon, my Jumento and me.

24

The journey grew long but Feliciano's stories helped me forget my fatigue. My feet were swollen from walking so much and I lost count of how many days we had been on the road. All that mattered was how many days were left: four, he told me. In four days we'll be there, doña. Tomorrow we'll wake up on the plains. You'll see how different everything is down there. There are no more rocks and everything from the ground comes up green. Then it's three days more on level ground that's mostly grass, it's very pleasant. You'll see the land yourself tomorrow when we wake up.

We were heading downhill, zigzagging down the slope. It was hard to hear each other on those switchbacks. Impossible to have a conversation. That's why I waited until night fell to be able to speak. But that day we had to keep going even after the sun had set: we had to reach the stream that separated the mountains from the grasslands. We arrived exhausted, with no energy to talk. I managed to ask him about this Ofelia he had been telling me about. I'll tell you more about her tomorrow, doña. Let's rest now, it's late.

And so we slept, that night, beside the stream, and while I slept I smelled a new scent in the air. I had never smelled anything like it before. The next day, when we awoke, I asked him where that scent came from.

He told me that it was the smell of dew: that's what dew smells like, doña, wet grass.

25

I don't want to hear it, mother. The poor donkey's doing his best. Remember how heavy his burden is, how steep the ground. Sometimes we spend the whole day going in circles, looking for a pass. And the reason we've got this problem, mother, is because I wasn't going to leave you behind. So don't complain; we're making progress. It'll be slow going, but I think you'll agree that's better than nothing. I already promised, mother, that when we find Lina we'll all go back. If God wills it. And if Lina wills it, too. Be patient, mother. Look at father, so quiet, not a complaint in the world. But you, you're reminding me of my Lina. Have pity on me. The path is steep. And remember, we wouldn't be here at all if I hadn't been born in such a miserable place. Be patient, and we'll end up somewhere better.

When mother got mad like that, I'd just talk to my donkey. Look at her, I'd tell him. She gets so mad, says she's tired of so much wandering. But she doesn't have to move a muscle; we're the ones doing all the work. I don't know what she has to complain about, Jumento. That's how I talked to my donkey when my mother started whining. And he was good to me. Not once did he turn his ear. At times I'd tell him how much I wanted to go and shout at the old witch who'd gotten us into this mess looking for the stream. What stream was she talking about, Jumento. There's no stream anywhere. And my donkey listened intently, and looked at me with those eyes of his, so full of understanding, and kept on walking. What a good donkey I'd gotten. Such a good listener. And so steadfast.

26

I don't know if it was my exhaustion from all those days on foot or the relief of knowing that we were nearing our destination, but that morning Feliciano had to wake me, though normally I was the one who had been getting up and waiting for him to awaken. So he came over to wake me and when I opened my eyes I couldn't believe what I was seeing: the sky was broad and low, almost on top of the earth, and there was so much grass that you couldn't see it all at once. Here, there, and everywhere you looked the ground was green, and the sky just kept on going, farther and farther, all the way to where it met the earth. I pointed this out to Feliciano. That's the horizon, doña. That's where we're going.

27

That day, around noon, I saw my donkey start walking straight ahead, purpose in his eyes. For days we'd been going in circles, looking for a way down. Until that day, when all of a sudden Jumento started to walk as if he knew where he was going. I left him to it and after a while the ground started to slope downwards. My donkey spent the whole day picking down the mountain. I tried to stop him at one point, because night was beginning to fall, but he wasn't happy about that and he pulled and pulled. He made it very clear that he didn't want us to stop there. I hesitated, but in the end I let him do what he thought was right. And that was how, late that night, we came to the stream. I couldn't believe it. Jumento didn't even wait for me to unhook him from the wagon. He went straight for the stream and lowered his head to quench his thirst. Even Christ could not have moved him from the spot. I unfastened the wagon and he kept on drinking. You sure were thirsty, Jumento, I said. He didn't even look at me. He just kept drinking. And I went to drink too, next to him. The water was fresh and it made me want to stay and soak for a while. The night was dark. I could barely see two feet in front of me but it didn't matter. I took off my clothes and got into the water to soak awhile. It was wonderful. After a while Jumento's thirst was quenched, and I gave him his food, and I told my parents. We made it, mother. We made it, father. To the stream.

On the plains you don't have to look where you're step-ping, your feet just start walking on their own, without anyone telling them where to step. Feliciano gathered our things while the donkey drank its fill in the stream. I told him I was going to look around a little bit, I wanted to check out these flat lands. Feliciano stood there star-ing at me and I took off like a shot before he could answer, overjoyed, my feet running of their own accord until I threw myself down on the grass and my back felt its softness and my eyes locked on that huge sky and I felt my heart racing and I was so happy that I couldn't close my mouth for smiling. It took me a while to calm down. Then I stood up and walked back to where Feliciano was, a little embarrassed. I thanked him.

"Don't worry, doña; I also had to run around the first time I saw this land."

"You really see how big the sky is here, don't you think?"

"Yes, señora, it's big."

"They told me the sea is big, too, have you seen it?"

"No, señora, I never have."

"Could it be as wide as this plain?"

"I have no idea, señora, but we should start moving because it's getting late."

So we began walking. My eyes couldn't get enough of that sky all day.

29

The next morning, I awoke to a strange noise. I opened my eyes and saw Jumento, next to me, and two boys climbing on the wagon. I yelled at them to get down from there: what the hell do you think you're doing. They hurried down and stayed silent, staring at the ground. They had two fishing rods with them. We're going fishing, they said. Where are you going to fish, I asked, there's nothing in this stream. If you keep going, señor, over where the mountains end, there's a lake. But where do the mountains end, I asked, they seem like they go on forever. Up ahead, señor, it opens up really wide. There's a lake there, sometimes. It's a dry lake, doesn't usually have any water, but just yesterday we heard it filled up. We're going to see if we can catch anything. We're sorry about climbing on your wagon, señor. We've just never seen a box as big as the ones you've got there. What are they for, señor. I told them I used them to trap kids who climbed on my wagon. That was all I had to say for them to take off running as if they were possessed by the devil, fishing rods wobbling in the air, along the edge of the stream.

As soon as I lost sight of them, I said to Jumento: come on, donkey, let's go see that lake.

My excitement grew the closer we got. We only had one day left: we'll get there tomorrow, doña. That's what Feliciano told me as soon as we were awake. I was so curious I couldn't stand it. I kept asking him to tell me more: please, tell me about Doña Ofelia, tell me about her crazy sons, tell me about Luis, tell me about the people that work for them, please. I kept on asking him, over and over. And bit by bit Feliciano shared stories about this or that, which made me try to imagine those people even more: Doña Ofelia got sick, she was wandering around ranting, that's what the ranch hands told me. And she had been such an even-tempered woman. They say she came into the kitchen early one morning, singing joyfully, dreamily, dressed all in white as usual but her red hair was completely disheveled. These days they say she sits in a chair, unmoving, for weeks at a time until she returns to reality. Some say she's been like that since her son José lost his mind, the one she adored so much. Others say she was like that because her husband got with almost every woman he came across and she was so furious about it she retreated into a world of her own. And they say that the only one who knows how to help her is a witch who comes to look after her. Her name is Iris. They say Iris knows how to treat her, that it takes some time, but she makes her well again. Doña Ofelia gave birth to nine sons. Half of them were sane and the other half were crazy. They call the crazy ones the Furies. They went crazy, one by one, around the age of fourteen, as if it had been predestined. Four of them. I saw them once when they were having one of their episodes. You've never seen anything like it. Their strength could destroy mountains. All the ranch hands have to go out together and catch them and sometimes even that's not enough. I saw this with my own eyes. It takes four or five determined ranch hands to hold down one of those crazies when they're going wild. And when they manage to catch them they tie them up in the stables until they calm down. The ranch hands are sick and tired of these rampages, but they have to put up with them because they keep on happening. And when it happens the father or one of the sane sons goes to fetch the doctor. And when the doctor arrives he gives them some kind of medicine that leaves them drooling. I haven't ever seen that with my own eyes, that's what the ranch hands tell me. You'll see this world yourself, tomorrow.

31

When we arrived at the lake, me and Jumento and my parents, I wanted nothing more than to give those kids hell. The whole thing was completely dry, not a single drop of water, just a bunch of rocks there between the mountains. It was like we were standing inside a giant pit in the earth. For a while I just stared out at the vast emptiness before my eyes. The silence was deep in that place. Even the sound of my breath had become an expanse. Not a whiff of air moved around me. It was as if everything had stopped. And then there was a scream. And another. And the screams began to reverberate around the pit, multiplying from every direction. And then all of a sudden I saw them again, those kids. They were launching rocks with slingshots, as if they were trying to hunt some animal. I yelled at them, what the hell are you doing. My voice hung in the air like theirs, repeating itself. We're hunting birds, they said. Liars. How can you be hunting birds when there aren't any birds around here. But they kept at it, with their slingshots, hunting their imaginary birds. I went back to Jumento, feeling sorry for myself, for having really believed in the lake. Then I heard the echo of a scream and raised my eyes and saw one of the kids sprinting toward the other one. He'd hit him on the head with a rock. There was a lot of blood. He started toward me, supporting the other one's head on his shoulder. He's my brother, he said. I asked them where we could find help. Let's go to our house: up ahead, alongside the lake, there's a path that leads to our house. I repeated this back to Jumento: come on, donkey, let's go alongside the lake. So I got them up on the wagon and we set off. The kid was still bleeding. When we got to the house, we were greeted by a bearded man. Father, said the uninjured boy, I'm sorry for bringing my brother home hurt like this. And the father, without thanking me for bringing them home, in fact barely even looking at me, grabbed the kid by the ear and carried him off into a cage in the back, yelling: and you'll stay there until your brother gets better. And then he pulled his wounded son off me and carried him to the cage too. This'll teach you not to get into mischief again, he told them, and then went back into the house. He didn't come to say goodbye to me or anything. I was just standing there, next to the wagon, filled with rage and a strong desire to punch the father in the face. Before leaving, I yelled out that he was never going to heal his wounded son or teach the other son a lesson like that. Then I told Jumento we were leaving. Come on, Jumento, let's get the hell out of this place.

32

Feliciano stopped to show me. Look, doña, we're close. He pointed to a long line of trees up ahead of us. That's the main gate, where you go in. Soon we were among those trees and my legs started to shake. I remembered what Balbina said: if they had work for me, I should stay, and if not, I should return to where I came from. The sounds I heard as soon as we passed through the gate were surprising. So much chirping. From what seemed like different kinds of birds. I looked up but couldn't see them anywhere. Those trees were so tall that the sky looked like it had been hemmed in again. We walked along that road quite a way until we came to a clearing. You could see a little more from there. Feliciano explained: what you see in front of you is the Loprete ranch. That's where Don Luis and Doña Ofelia and all their sons live. If you look carefully, you can see the stables in the distance. Beyond that, the ranch hands' quarters. And beyond that, the chicken coop, the goat pens, the storage sheds. And in the far distance the hills. Don't be overwhelmed by all this, doña. If you start to feel like that, look away and stare into the distance. You'll see how everything here is surrounded by land. Don't forget that, doña. Always look to the horizon, as far as you can, and remember that you're going to the sea.

33

We went back, me and Jumento, to the empty lake. I was still so angry. The sun was as hot as ever: it couldn't have been later than three. I sat beside the lake, staring blankly at the dried roots along its edge. What a strange place, Lina. If you could see it. You should be here, with me, seeing all this. Wherever you are, wherever you've gone to. And as I was lost in thought, I heard Jumento take off. He had the wagon and my parents and everything, leaving me sitting there alone. I gave him a quick whistle, to get him to stop. He listened. Such good manners, my Jumento. I got up on the wagon and he started off again, as if he knew where he was going and I was just along for the ride: all right, Jumento, let's go wherever you want to go. And so he did, for several hours, walking confidently, until we came to a stream. It looked like a different stream, wider and more generous than the one from before. Jumento lowered his head to drink, so thirsty, not another care in the world. I got down from the wagon to do the same. You really wanted to get to the water, I told him, and I started drinking too. Then I took off my clothes and got in to bathe in those waters. It was cold. I wondered if we were in a different part of the same stream or if this was a new one, and if Lina had followed these waters or the others. I looked up, the sky tinged sunset-purple: we would spend the night in that spot. I got out of the stream and went back to thanking Jumento and watching him drink his water.

34

And that's how we, Feliciano and I, arrived in that place. He introduced me to Gregorio first. He was the ranch hand who had been there longest, he said. Her name is Lina, she's from the quebrada, I brought her with me because she's looking for work. The ranch hand immediately went to find his wife and told her the same thing: that I was from the quebrada and I was looking for work. The wife asked me what I knew how to do. I told her I knew how to cook and knit and that I could also learn to do anything else they needed. She said to her husband: I think they're looking for a cook at the house. Feliciano explained that there were two kinds of work here: indoors and outdoors. Outdoors on the land and indoors in the house. That's what she said, and though I didn't really understand much, I looked at the ranch hand's wife and told her that I wasn't picky: I was fine with cooking or anything else. And she left quickly to go and ask. I stood there between Feliciano and the husband and stared into space, just waiting. They began to talk. This Gregorio filled him in on the news, he seemed happy to see Feliciano again. It hadn't even been half an hour before I saw the woman coming back. This time she spoke to me: yes, doña, there's a job for you in the house, working in the kitchen, serving the family; they want to meet you. I looked at Feliciano. Go ahead, he said. Good luck.

35

I'm not sure what happened, but I woke up in the middle of the night, before the first rays of sun, still not a hint of dawn in the sky. My donkey slept standing, next to me. But the stream was more awake even than before. It cascaded down as if a great rain had flooded its insides and it needed to get it all out, such a fury of water. Maybe all that noise, like a rumbling stomach, was what had woken me up. There was no other sound, just that roar of water crashing on rocks. I looked at Jumento and looked at the wagon and looked at my parents and wondered what I was doing there: what are you doing here, Cruz, tramping around with donkeys and wagons and coffins and open sky with absolutely no idea where you're going. Where are you going to go today, Cruz. You don't even have the slightest idea where your Lina could be. I never saw myself getting into such a mess. That's how I was feeling, all sorry for myself, when I remembered the old woman Octavia's words: that I should follow the water. I listened once more to the fury of that stream and it gave me hope, that it was really going somewhere. I couldn't see the water itself, just the white of its foam, in that dark hour before dawn. The sky was up there, still untouched by the glow of morning. I stood, just listening to the sound and waiting for the sun to rise.

36

If only you could see me, Octavia. I've been working in this kitchen for three weeks and I'm still not used to this place. There are eleven of them, each with their own brand of crazy. Don Luis, Doña Ofelia, and their nine sons. They gave me a job in the kitchen and cleaning the house, too, because they say the woman who did the cleaning left. Apparently one of the sons was harassing her. She got tired of it and split. I need your medicines to feel better, Octavia, I'm exhausted from getting used to so many new things, on top of the fatigue of the journey. Luckily, Gregorio's wife is kind to me. Her name is Alda. Sometimes she comes to help out or she makes dinner so I can go to bed early. They gave me a bedroom off the kitchen. She sleeps with her husband in the quarters for the ranch hands: it's a huge house, with six bedrooms for everyone, married and unmarried. Feliciano keeps introducing me to new people, but I swear, Octavia, it's hard work to remember all these new faces. And I have enough to do already, just dealing with the family's crazy ways. I don't know which of them lost their mind first, but all of them are off their rockers. They make a distinction between the sane ones and the crazy ones, but I swear to you, there's not a sane person in this house. When I see Feliciano, I tell him that I'm dizzy from all the people and all the craziness. And he laughs. He tells me not to complain: just try not to go crazy yourself, doña. Sometimes when I get off work early I go and eat with the ranch hands. They laugh a lot on this ranch. I think they laugh so much because they're working outdoors, not inside with this family. One time Gregorio laughed so hard he cried. He had found one of the crazies screwing a she-goat in the corral that afternoon. And the lunatic had even named the goat. Pepa, he said he called it. And he was declaring his love for it and serenading it. And Gregorio kept laughing while he told this story while he drank his wine. One of those nights I learned that it was true that they had been harassing the cleaning woman. That was really why she left. And they also told me that the cook was very old and unwell and that she had died not long before I arrived. That was why I got the job. Although I used to complain about my empty skies and my boring days, I can assure you, Octavia, it's impossible to get bored here. No two days are alike. I've never seen so much commotion. This place is too big and there are too many people and it's all too much. Now I understand what Feliciano meant back when we arrived and he said: it's all too much. But I only recently understood. Before one thing has ended something else has begun. And the crickets here will deafen you, but the dogs never bark. I noticed that the other day. I think they can no longer be bothered. If they barked at everything they saw, the poor things would be barking all day. That must be why they're always lying around, giving everything the side-eye. I swear to you, Octavia, there's so much going on here it's exhausting. Maybe I should do like those dogs and stop looking around so much.

37

Jumento started drinking from the stream again, as soon as he woke up. I went over to tell him: today we have to keep going in the direction of the water, Jumento, just like Octavia said. You don't have to worry, because we're going to walk along the stream the whole way. I promise, you won't go thirsty again. Jumento looked at me and seemed to understand. He settled, waiting for me to hitch him up to the wagon. And after I hitched him up, we set off, that morning, at dawn. As we progressed, the stream's fury grew, as if the weight it carried on its back only filled it with more confidence. I looked at Jumento and said: we must be heading downhill, because this stream is really getting bold now. Jumento didn't say anything and kept on walking. Around midday I told him to stop for a while, to rest a bit, to eat something. I gave him his hay. We were there, resting, when we saw the women coming with their goats. There were two women, and each was coming down with her own goat. As soon as they came to the stream, I went over to them: I'm sorry to bother you, señoras, but I'm lost. I'm not from these parts. I was too ashamed to tell them that I was looking for my wife or that I was looking for the sea. I stopped talking and waited for them to say something. What can we do for you, señor, said the older one. And then it just came out of me all at once: I'm looking for my wife, her name is Lina. And how surprised was I when the older one turned to the other and asked if she remembered Lina: that woman who was looking for the sea. And when I heard that, I couldn't stay silent anymore: that's her, I said. She went that way, señor. Following the water. That was what the older one told me. I was filled with such hope that I couldn't contain myself: and when did you see her, if you don't mind me asking. They looked at each other, trying to remember, and then they started to have a conversation. I watched as their eyes looked this way and that, and left them alone to think about the question until they came to an agreement: a while ago now, señor. Maybe six weeks or more. I thanked them and went back to my wagon: mother, father, we're falling behind. We have to get moving.

38

I saw her arrive that morning and my eyes couldn't believe what they were seeing. Hermelinda had shown up in this part of the world. I remembered those women with their goats who wanted to find her a job. I don't know which of us was more surprised. As soon as she saw me she said, but you were going to the sea. We only had time to greet each other with a nod before Alda took her inside to introduce her. Doña Ofelia received her, asking what she knew how to do. She said she knew a lot about goats, how to milk them, how to make cheese. They could have sent her to work in the corral with the goats but they needed help in the house so they asked her to work with me. When she told me that they'd given her a job, I embraced her like she was my own sister. In the beginning she was as lost as I had been, so I gave her the advice that Feliciano had given me: it's all too much here; don't get overwhelmed, Hermelinda, and always keep your eyes on the horizon, as far as you can see.

39

My spirits had lifted since meeting the goat women. They'd seen Lina, and that gave me an unfamiliar kind of strength. That feeling of lostness had gone away. Jumento caught me singing every now and then, and he'd just stare at me from beneath those long eyelashes of his. I told him: look, donkey, I'm just happy. That's all. So we continued alongside the stream. And there were days when we didn't cross paths with a single soul. But I didn't care, because I could feel that we were on the right track. That's what I told them, my parents: mother, father, we're on the right track. Those women saw her, so we're doing all right, on our way to the sea. And so we kept going, the four of us, following the stream until we met the goatherds. I was so confident that I didn't even hesitate for a second before asking them: had they seen a woman looking for the sea. I wasn't embarrassed to ask anymore, everything was going so well, so I said it just like that. But they seemed confused, and that rattled me a bit. I stood there, not really knowing what to say, waiting for them to speak. They looked at each other, stupefied, and stayed like that for a while until one of them came around: it must have been that woman who was out here looking for a river. And immediately I said yes, that was her. And so they added that they'd seen a woman who looked like she was starving, and that she'd collapsed, right there, and that they'd brought her to Balbina's house, to take care of her. I listened to their story and nearly dropped to my knees to kiss their feet. I clasped my hands in prayer, begging them: please, please take me to Balbina.

I didn't see much of Feliciano. He worked outdoors, with the horses. I had started to think that working outside might be a little less stressful than working indoors. I don't know. Maybe not. Maybe it was just the way I felt trapped in that house and all its craziness. Surrounded by shrieking, the hours were endless in there. Luckily I had Hermelinda for company. Sometimes I tried not to hear what was going on, but your ears aren't like your eyes, you can't just close them. And they shrieked round the clock. Some louder than others. Sometimes it was the crazies, whose screams tore you apart. Or the tyrannical sane ones. Or the master, who'd had enough. Or Doña Ofelia mumbling her litany. Lord knows who she was speaking to. These sounds were with me all day and pursued me throughout the night. They echoed in my head when I was lying on my cot in the darkness. The only thing that calmed me was remembering my empty sky and my boring days at home with Cruz. I don't know if it was homesickness. I'm not sure. Perhaps it wasn't longing, it was just my head exploding from all that shrieking.

41

They looked at me suspiciously. I don't know if it was the wagon or the coffins, but I looked right back at them and didn't give anything away: I wasn't about to go telling everyone about what I was carrying. They hesitated a bit and my breath caught in my throat as I waited for them to say something. But there was nothing doing: the goatherds looked at me and then turned their eyes to the wagon. I started to get uncomfortable, but I stuck to my silence. I didn't want to go around explaining things; I just wanted them to take me to this Balbina woman. But I could tell they weren't about to help, because they wouldn't stop looking at the wagon. Finally, I said: I have my parents with me. They were silent, not saying a word. I clarified: I'm bringing them with me because you can't abandon your dead. They looked at me warily and told me they didn't remember any Balbina: we have no idea where this Balbina lives. That's what they told me, before they went on their way and left us there, me and my donkey and my wagon. I looked at my donkey and told him: those men didn't trust us, Jumento, we'll have to find Balbina on our own.

In these parts misfortune comes with the rains. That's what Alda said when I told her I wanted to see it rain. When you see it rain here, you won't want to see it again, Lina. The rain here is relentless: it takes hold like grief. Too many days of endless water, it doesn't stop. It ruins the land: mud everywhere that you can hardly walk in. Even the animals slip and slide in the mire, and sometimes we even lose them to the watering hole. They float feet up and then we never see them again. And the rains arrive with terrifying lightning. No, Lina, when you see it rain you'll wish it would never rain again. That's what Alda told me, and I didn't know what to make of it. I couldn't imagine such a thing. It happened one night when we were at the ranch hands' quarters. They were playing cards and I was with Hermelinda and Alda. Hermelinda was telling us that Olegario was sweet on her. He was the youngest ranch hand, and he kept seeking her out. And it seemed to me that she liked him. The thing is that it made you feel happy just seeing them together. That boy was as absurdly attractive as she was. Neither of them looked like they belonged to this world. And she was telling us that Olegario had told her earlier in the day that you could see in the sky that the rains were coming. And right then we heard a noise that sounded like the earth was splitting in two. Everyone ran outside: they wanted to see the lightning, they said. I joined them. In my lifetime I had never witnessed such a thing. The sky shook, convulsing, and filled with cracks like wounds of light. And with each crack the ranch hands' faces lit up in a flash and disappeared again. And we all stayed outside watching this spectacle. Then we heard some noises that sounded like they would shatter the sky into pieces. And I had been so angry at God for so long that I didn't pray for anything anymore, but the din was so loud that I was tempted to ask him to stop being so angry. And then the first fat drops started to fall. And the downpour began.

43

So we left, me and Jumento, heading nowhere in particular, to look for Balbina. Which way do we go, donkey, which way to find Balbina. So that was how we got going, that day. And Jumento looked at me, always so thoughtful, as if he cared where we were going, as if it would mean something to him to find my Lina. I have no idea which way Jumento took me that day. I just let him take me. For a while already I hadn't known what to tell him. So I just left him to it, because I liked how persistent he was, that donkey. Let's just go find Balbina, I said. And Jumento got moving. I walked behind him, with what little family I had, and said: look at this beautiful landscape, mother. Or: what a difficult journey this has been, father. Or: where could Lina be, mother. Or: just a little longer, father, just hold on a little longer and then we can rest. Those were the kinds of things I told them, while Jumento led us forward as if he knew where he was going.

44

Doña Ofelia became much worse with the rains. Her sons began calling for me right away to go and see her. When I found her she was a wreck. Sitting in her rocking chair, scrawny and delirious. She was whispering random words to lord knows who. At times it seemed like she was talking to someone; at times more like she was talking to herself. Once in a while she heaved a sigh, then continued whispering and rocking. That's it. How was I supposed to help her. I looked at them, at Don Luis and his son Luis, and told them I had no idea what to do. They immediately started to argue. We ought to get Iris to make her better; we can't go get that witch in this pouring rain; she may be a witch but she's the only one who can help; the rain is too heavy, we should wait till tomorrow; it doesn't make any sense to wait, it will still be raining tomorrow; and whether the father or the son or one of the ranch hands would go. They argued like that for a good while until the father lost his temper and began shouting that he'd had it with all of them and that he would go fetch the witch himself. I was still next to Doña Ofelia and I was getting more and more nervous. The noise from the storm on top of seeing Doña Ofelia like that had been upsetting enough. I was already so frightened. It seemed like she had lost her mind when the thunder started. And then the shouting match on top of it all. In the end Don Luis went alone, and the son asked me to stay with his mother until Doña Iris arrived. I brought her tea and sat with her. I spoke to her gently. I said that Iris was on the way, but she didn't seem to hear. Her eyes were blank, like she was looking inward, and she was still babbling. That was it. It terrified me to see her blank stare. Hang on, Lina, help is coming. That's what I was thinking. And it was around two hours before the son called me to say that Doña Iris was in the hall and I should go and get her and bring her to Doña Ofelia. I went to greet her. The woman was drenched but what struck me more was her size. She was tiny, all sinew and bone. Like there was nothing else to her. And her eyes had an intensity that seemed like they could wound you. I didn't even want to look at her, she frightened me so much. I took her straight to Doña Ofelia's room, casting my eyes to the floor as if I were doing penance. When we got to the room she grabbed my arm and forced me to look at her: it took a lot of determination for you to get here, don't walk around staring at the floor like that. That's what she told me. I nearly fainted. There was something about that woman's eyes. She could see straight through you. I was dumbstruck. She rummaged around in the bag she was holding and pulled out some dry leaves. Take these, she said; make yourself some tea and go rest.

45

Jumento turned away from the water and started to climb the hill. I stopped him. I bent down to ask him what he was doing: you're heading away from the stream, Jumento, are you sure you know what you're doing? And Jumento looked at me all calm and untroubled. And I realized he really did know what he was doing, so I agreed to let him do it: all right, if you're sure, let's go. So Jumento went up and up. And we reached a sort of town. There were just six or seven houses. That was where he stopped, Jumento, stock-still. So I got down from the wagon and counted the houses: there were so few that I decided to go and ask one by one. And they told me things like: up ahead, over there, next door. I was already on the fifth house and a little short on hope when a kind woman answered the door. I asked after Balbina. That's me, she said. And I got so nervous I nearly collapsed. Good afternoon, I said, I'm Lina's husband. I was told she had come this way, heading for the sea. I'm very sorry to bother you, but I miss my wife and I'm looking for her. This Balbina woman stood silent. So I told her not to worry, that she would tell me if she felt like telling me and if she didn't, that was fine too.

46

A full day had passed since the storm. It was a day of steady rain, not tempestuous. Doña Ofelia was a little better; Doña Iris was still with her, keeping her company. I didn't have much work to do. I was in the kitchen with Hermelinda when they came to ask me for some soup for Doña Ofelia. I felt calm when I brought it to her. I wasn't as afraid of seeing Iris. Since she had given me those tea leaves, I didn't feel as tense inside. And I felt more rested. And I enjoyed watching the steady rain and smelling the wet earth. I even began to think that Cruz would have enjoyed seeing the rain, too, instead of staying put in our barren land. I entered the room, careful not to make much noise, unsure of what I would find. I immediately saw Doña Ofelia in her chair. Her eyes looked a little less lost. She was looking directly at Doña Iris, silent. You have to hold Doña Iris's gaze. And Doña Ofelia did, without lowering her eyes. Eventually she said: may lightning strike him down. I don't know whether she was talking about her husband, but that's what she said. I heard her clearly: may lightning strike him down. I put the soup on the table and was leaving when Doña Iris looked at me: there are ill-fated days ahead, take care. I returned to the kitchen. As soon as I walked through the door Hermelinda asked me if Doña Ofelia was saying that Don

Luis should be struck by lightning. I nodded. We both looked out the window: it was not a stormy day. No lightning, no thunder, nothing. Just a peaceful rain that kept on falling effortlessly. Then I said to Hermelinda: the witch says there are ill-fated days ahead. And Hermelinda thought it was funny and laughed and told me that the previous night Olegario had proposed to her in the rain. Her impossible eyes dancing and her body shaking with laughter. I told her that it was a joy to see them together and that she should take his proposal seriously. It seems too soon, she said. Don't think that, I said, life passes quickly.

47

The woman hesitated for a moment. Maybe it wasn't that long, but to me it seemed endless. Soon her husband appeared, to ask her what was going on. She didn't keep anything from him. She told him: this man is looking for Lina, the woman who was on her way to the sea. And who is he, if I might ask. He says he's her husband. Balbina excused herself and left me standing at the door. I could hear what they were saying inside anyway. After a while they came back, the two of them. They asked how I could prove that I was the husband of the woman they'd met. I stood there a few seconds in silence. I looked at Jumento: he was eating some grass from the ground. The couple was still there, peering out the door. I looked at them again. I didn't know what to tell them. So I told them the truth: I have no idea how to prove it, but Lina is my wife and I'm sure of that. If she weren't my wife, I wouldn't be traipsing all over creation with this donkey, dragging my parents behind me. I'd be in my house, with my Lina, and I wouldn't be wandering around out here looking for her.

48

When I awoke the next day it sounded like all hell had broken loose in the stables. I dressed quickly and went to see what was going on. When I stepped outside I ran into Gregorio who was yelling for the ranch hands. I ran to the stalls and there they all were, scrambling and grabbing knives. The crazies were a little way off, running around in the rain in a fit of fury. The ranch hands began chasing after them and the crazies attacked like wild dogs. And then we heard one of them begin to howl like an animal and the others responded with piercing screams, like they were speaking in some mangled language, and I stood there with the other women watching them as this battle raged in the rain; and then Feliciano walked past me and said: always the same, their rage is reborn with the rain. And I saw him going to help Gregorio who was trying to catch one of the crazies, but it was impossible: the madman kept escaping with ease. At one point three of them were trying to restrain him and they still couldn't. The madman shook with such force that ranch hands went flying, landing spread-eagled in the mud, like sacks of bones. Then Don Luis arrived to see what was happening and put his head in his hands. Just you wait, they'll bring out the boleadoras and that will be the end of it, Alda said. And then one of the brothers or

Don Luis himself will go fetch the doctor, wait and see. And that's exactly what happened. It was impossible to control the rage of those four crazies who were running around like maniacs and shrieking like they were possessed. Eventually the ranch hands went out on horseback with the boleadoras to hunt them down one by one and bring them back to the stables all bruised, and chain them up until the doctor arrived. I couldn't believe what I was seeing. The ranch hands came back bloody and covered in mud. Gregorio had one hand torn open, it looked like he had been bitten by a rabid dog. Alda went inside the house to find some bandages. Hermelinda was standing beside me, pale and mute, her eyes wide in shock. I must have looked the same: it was the first time that we had seen anything like it. Alda was treating Gregorio's wound when Don Luis came by to rebuke us. What was I doing there, outside with Hermelinda, our jobs were inside the house and they were looking for us. I returned to the house, following Don Luis, and Hermelinda followed me. What they wanted was their lunch. The five sane sons were already sitting at the table and Don Luis sat down at the head, waiting for us to bring him his food. We rushed to the kitchen while the six of them began to argue again. They didn't care that we could hear everything. They didn't spare us a single one of their complaints. I had seen the big storm a few nights ago, and Doña Ofelia's derangement, and the witch's eyes which I couldn't forget and the rampaging lunatics and on top of all that I had to hear Don Luis's litany of complaints. The man was exhausted. He began by telling them, his sons, that he couldn't stand them anymore, not a single one of them: not the lunatics, who were a lost cause, and not the ones around the table either because they were all good-for-nothings. And what would happen to this land when he was no longer around. And that it was their fault his wife had lost her mind. And that he couldn't stand her, Doña Ofelia, anymore either, with these episodes that left her raving in her chair. He couldn't stand the mayhem anymore, he said, shouting at them as if he were settling an old score. It's true that everything was screwed up, but it hadn't happened overnight. I still wonder which of them went crazy first. I'll ask Alda, she knows everything. I was in the kitchen and lunch was ready but I didn't want to go out and serve it. But I pulled myself together and went out with the tray laid with the food and right then I heard Don Luis telling them that since the storm a few nights ago he couldn't sleep, it was his wife's fault, and that he hadn't slept last night either because of the lunatics and that he was going to go take a nap and that if one of them hadn't gone to fetch the doctor by nightfall then he would have to be the one to get him. So he went to take his siesta, Don Luis, while his kids remained at the table for much of the afternoon, blaming each other for what they hadn't done. Then they went to see the ranch hands and they visited the stables to check on the lunatics. They were howling and bruised and injuring themselves more by trying to break free from the chains. By that time it was getting dark. Don Luis woke up and saw that none of his kids had gone to fetch the doctor. They got caught in another hellish argument again, and by this time I was dazed from all the shouting. His kids wanted him to stay, but Don Luis was too furious that night. He asked for his mare and left to go get the doctor. No sooner had he gone than a storm broke out, one that seemed like it would split the earth in two forever. And then we saw Luis go after his father to try to catch him. The thunder made me want to crawl under my bed, but I remembered Doña Iris: I needed to stay alert; ill-fated days were ahead.

Finally, they seemed to accept the idea that I might be Lina's husband, and they invited me in. I told Jumento to wait for me outside: I'll be right back, Jumento. The donkey stopped chewing and looked at me. I nodded and he went back to his grass. Then I went inside. They offered me a little water and started to tell me what happened. That they found Lina on the verge of fainting by the edge of the stream. That a friend had come to revive her. That she told them she wanted to see the sea. That they suggested she find some work for a while first, because she'd never make it to the sea in that state. That Lina agreed. And that a goatherd took her away, to a ranch, to look for work. I listened very carefully. In the end, I said: I'll have to change my plans. I'm not going to the sea anymore. Now I have to go to that ranch. Tell me, please, where I might find it.

I heard about it the next morning, as soon as I woke up. The house had become a hive of demons. Everyone was running around like a pack of wild dogs that had lost its leader. Hermelinda told me: Don Luis died when he went to fetch the doctor. They're saying he was struck by lightning on the high bridge. His body all black and shrunken. Luis says his father was crossing the bridge when the lightning hit. That he saw it from afar. And that it was a direct strike. That he heard a sound like a launching flare and saw a light as bright as the sun on a cloudless day. And at the same moment his horse fell to the ground, bringing him down, too. And when he reached his father he found a blackened, child-sized body, like it was made of coal, beside the mare.

Some said he sacrificed himself, that the man couldn't take any more insanity. Others said it was the witch and crossed themselves, afraid that Doña Iris might make another evil wish come true. That day was hell. Doña Ofelia stayed shut in her room with Iris and no one dared tell them the news. Eventually Luis went in to see her. He found her rocking in her chair with that blank look: father is dead, he told her. But it seemed like she didn't hear. She continued rocking, lost in her world. By that time all the sane sons knew. The crazy ones were still in chains in the stables. They sent Olegario to fetch the doctor to treat the crazies and Luis asked Gregorio to go into town to find the carpenter and ask him to make a coffin, an emergency, that's what he said, so Gregorio sped off in search of the carpenter. Meanwhile Luis took the cart and two of the ranch hands to the high bridge to find those chunks of coal: all that remained of his father. The doctor was first to arrive, he went to see the crazies and gave them their injections that left them drooling. They were taken from the stables and put in the tool shed. Then the cart with Don Luis's remains arrived. They say they just left the mare in the field beside the bridge. And then Gregorio arrived with the carpenter. Apparently the man always came whenever there was work and they asked for him. The whole town had heard about how Don Luis had died. We were asked to prepare some food for the burial. We were cooking from noon onward, Hermelinda and I. The kitchen was abuzz with people telling stories to each other. By six that evening Don Luis was in the coffin and people from town began to arrive. They told us: everyone's coming from town for the wake. Some of them were worried because Don Luis had given them jobs they were afraid of losing; others were sorry and said that he was a good man who had to deal with too many problems; others were angry, saying that he was a cold and unpleasant man who had done bad things; others were so surprised their eyes were popping out of their heads, and one of them even said good riddance, he was a bastard and he's finally dead. We heard it all in the fields that afternoon, in the commotion caused by his death. At some point Luis came into the kitchen to tell us that lots of people had arrived and was the food ready. We told him it was. He gave us instructions: the rain had stopped so we'd hold the wake in the open air near the hill where their dead were buried. That we should ask Gregorio to bring us to the hill in the cart. That we should wear mourning dress. That we should bring the trestles and boards and the linen tablecloths.

They told me I couldn't keep on going how I'd been going so far. That I'd have to make a decision. The path went over the high mountains until it reached the hills and then over the hills until it arrived at the ranch. There was no way, with the wagon, to cross those mountains. You've come all the way from the quebrada and it must have taken a lot for you to get here with your wagon and all, but from here on, there's no way. You'll have to leave it behind if you want to make it to the ranch. I asked for a moment alone, to consider. I left the house and met my donkey, who was waiting for me. What are we going to do, Jumento. We can't keep going with the wagon. What am I going to do with my parents. And he looked at me thoughtfully, with a kind of calm only a donkey could have, and I understood everything. I went back to knock on the door. They invited me in again. I told them: I have no house to go back to, all I can do is go on.

They helped me put my parents into two big sacks. They helped me load the bones onto my donkey. And then we left, me and Jumento, to face those mountains.

It was night by the time everything was ready: the tables, the food, the family, the doctor, the people, the ranch hands, the two of us, and the priest. And there was a mass with the coffin and all the people talking and all the food on the tables. I went over to the coffin. It was a beautiful coffin, well-made. People ate while the night went on without a single drop falling, as if the sky had known it needed to stop for a while so we could bury the master. Feliciano came up to me; you've had some difficult days, doña, I owe you an apology, I should never have brought you to this circus. I smiled at him: it's not your fault, it's the rain. And then Alda came over: I told you, misfortune comes with the rains. Who knows what things will be like now, without Don Luis. I went back to help Hermelinda at the tables, who was still serving people. She was speaking to a thin man. This is the carpenter, she said, he made the coffin. And I looked at him and froze, breathless, as if my heart had stopped. I had no doubt. I asked his name. I'm El Tala, he said, and the moment he said it his eyes filled with tears and I nodded and he hugged me and we stood there hugging each other as if the world would end that very night.

SECOND PART

From what ancient desert are you memory
That you thirst and in water waste away
And raise your corpse toward space
As if your water belonged to the sky?

ALFONSINA STORNI (TR. DAVID MASSE)

1

We were at Anselmo's that afternoon. It couldn't have been later than two: the sun was blazing when we laid eyes on him. The way he looked, it was like he could have turned to dust right there in front of us, as if his soul had been sucked out and all that remained were his skin and a few stubborn bones dragging his feet along. We saw him off in the distance, when El Tala looked up and stared at the approaching figure, lurching forward as if someone were shoving him along from behind. We remained seated, transfixed by the steadfast effort of that desiccated body, like wires wrapped in tanned hide.

When he got closer we could see his eyes; they looked so tired. Tulio stood to ask who he was. What brings you here, friend. And those eyes looked at him, at Tulio, as if they wanted to say why they had come but his tongue wouldn't move. El Tala offered him a little water. Have a few drops, brother, your throat must be parched. And then the man collapsed at Tulio's feet, as if the air in his lungs had left him all at once in that last step. El Tala's hand remained in the air a moment too long, holding the glass out in offering, as Tulio bent down first, followed by the rest of us, to get a closer look. His cheeks were gaunt, all protruding bone, and the rest of his face was sunken, shriveled. His eyes were still open. Tulio pressed his ear to the man's chest, not expecting much, and after listening awhile he said that no, friends, this guy is dead. And clearly he was right, because just a few moments later the first flies showed up, as if the rot had started before he'd even arrived.

2

We learned his name was Ramos soon after, but that evening we didn't know anything about the man who had come here only to fall to pieces at our feet. We spent days trying to figure out why that ruined husk who could barely walk for starvation had gone to the trouble of delivering his last breath to our doorstep. It occurred to El Tala, one afternoon, that we should go and ask Iris, the wizened old woman who knows about remedies and omens, to see if she might be able to tell us something about the man who had met his maker at Anselmo's. We went, El Tala and I, to knock on her door, but we found her outside with her donkey. Most likely she was just about to go to the Lopretes' farm, to look after Doña Ofelia. That was all she ever used the donkey for. She must have seen us coming out of the corner of her eye, and she waited for us, standing next to the animal.

Her rucksack hung from her shoulder. We quickened our pace and explained: we've come to ask you a question, Doña Iris. A man showed up at Anselmo's. We have no idea who he is. He collapsed in front of us before we had the opportunity to speak. We just buried him there, where he fell. Iris stared at us, silent, with those wrinkled eyes of hers. She adjusted the rucksack and, before climbing onto the donkey, nodded: come back tomorrow, she said, and we watched her tiny body trot off, toward the Lopretes'.

3

We went back the next day to see Doña Iris. This time
Anselmo came too, because he was fond of her.
When we got there, all three of us, there was no need
to announce our arrival. The door opened as soon as
we were near. I've been waiting for you, she said, and
invited us inside. She gestured: sit. We found a spot
on the floor. She remained standing and looked at
the three of us all together, but it was as if she were
looking at each of us alone. That was something
about Iris: she always had enough eyes for whoever
she needed to see. She stayed silent for a while, her
gaze still fixed on us, and we too remained silent, out
of respect, not saying a word. We didn't need to
remind her why we had come. The man is called
Ramos, she said, and as soon as she did we saw El
Tala bury his head in his hands. He was still, finger-
tips pressed into his black hair, and then a gasp came
out from his chest. It was thin, at first, but then it
started to take on weight, until it became a
full-throated cry. We didn't want to embarrass him.
We looked away and remained silent so El Tala could
let out whatever he needed to let out. And it continued that way, a long while, until he swallowed it back
down, as much as he could. He blinked, trying to
hide it, but his eyes were choking back tears too.
Doña Iris brought him some water: drink, she said.

And El Tala took a few sips with shaking hands that barely managed to find his mouth. We stayed a while longer, waiting for El Tala to come back to himself, before heading down toward Anselmo's.

4

We hadn't known El Tala's last name until then. But we learned it, that very same afternoon, after he had regained control of the air in his lungs. Iris's house was already far away, in the distance, when we heard El Tala speak, his voice clean, calm again, as he said: that man was like a father to me in the forest. He's my mother's brother. We couldn't speak. We took a few more steps downhill. Perhaps El Tala was waiting for a word from us, but we had no idea what to say. We didn't want him to lose control of his breath again. I looked at Anselmo, to see if anything had occurred to him, but he lowered his head and I knew it would be better to keep quiet. So that was how we walked home, the three of us, as the day came to a close. And the last rays of sun hit our backs, stretching our shadows along the path. Down below, where we lived, night had already fallen.

5

As soon as we got back to town, El Tala left for his house and we continued to Anselmo's. Tulio was there, waiting for us. We told him about Iris, and about Ramos, and we stayed talking until late that night. It seemed we knew very little about El Tala. We pulled together everything we had: about ten years' worth, ever since he'd first showed up. We'd seen him arrive at Anselmo's, one afternoon, his insides knotted from hunger. He could work with wood, that was the first thing he told us, and he had never seen a cow in his life. He looked at the cows like someone witnessing an apparition of the Virgin. Such a wide-open sky, he said, and so many cows. Where I come from, we don't have cows. We have ants, and snakes, and if you want to go anywhere at all you need sturdy boots and sharp eyes. Not like here, where you have cows and grass and you can walk without watching where you're going. I wouldn't be so sure, Tulio said, you've got to watch out, always watch where you're going. Look what happened to Anselmo, who didn't watch where he was going and ended up married to La Colorada. Those icy eyes of hers, the color of water. You can't even look at them for more than a second, can't talk back to them either, no way. In short, ten years had passed and we knew very little about El Tala. But he hadn't lied to us. He really did know how to work with wood. We'd seen his skill early on. The way he handled a chisel, it was like it was part of his own body, embedded into the flesh of his hands. Many went to him to learn, and he taught them all, little by little. But no one around here had a knack for the work the way El Tala did. Maybe some things can only be learned in the cradle. That was why, when the Lopretes wanted a job done well, they asked for him. And off he would go, El Tala, and there he would stay as long as necessary, until the work was done.

6

El Tala appeared at Anselmo's as the first stars were beginning to reveal themselves. We'd been sitting there with Tulio, outside, drinking gin. His steps were slow as we watched him draw near, his shoulders slumped. He acknowledged us with a nod and sat, or rather let himself fall, on the chair. Seeing him like that, I kept quiet, but Tulio was always a big talker, always knew how to fill the silence. I heard, he said. El Tala nodded, as Anselmo appeared with his gin. Anselmo set the glass on the table and rested a hand on El Tala's shoulder, as if to convey the sympathy he hadn't expressed the night before. The gesture seemed to remind El Tala of why he had come, because then he looked right at him, at Anselmo, and didn't waste another second: forgive me, Don Anselmo, but we can't just leave him like that, all nameless and unmarked. That man might as well have been my father. I have to give him a real burial. As I listened to him talk, I realized I wasn't very interested in going around digging up dead bodies, but I didn't say anything. The first to speak was Anselmo. Whatever you need, my Tala. And with that El Tala deflated with a long hard breath, and a look of pure relief washed over his eyes.

Anselmo got up to go back inside, excusing himself, and then El Tala got up to go as well: I'll come by tomorrow.

He downed the rest of the gin, and we watched him walk away, a sudden urgency in his stride, back home.

He's going to make the coffin, said Tulio, who never missed a beat.

7

And that was what happened. El Tala came the next day, in his wagon, with the freshly polished coffin. Don Anselmo had given us his instructions: dress in black, and leave El Tala be. He'd said we should come at seven. And there we were, Tulio, Anselmo, and I, all dressed in black and waiting for El Tala. The rains hadn't come yet, as luck would have it: we could still see where we had buried him, a few steps from the tables where we gathered to drink our gin, right where the good man had come to breathe his last breath. You could see the fresh earth. Anselmo had gotten us some shovels. He'd borrowed them from Fausto, who lived nearby and always had things in a pinch. When we got there, Anselmo asked us not to let El Tala lay a finger on that ground. So we didn't. Right away, El Tala offered to do the digging himself, but Anselmo raised his hand, palm open toward where El Tala stood, as if to say leave it to us, we'll dig him up, let us do this for you. Knowing El Tala, it must have been hard for him to accept. He didn't like going around receiving favors from people. He must have only said yes out of the feeling between them. Don Anselmo thought highly of El Tala, and El Tala respected Don Anselmo. And so on we went, as the sun fell, digging up the dead man.

We reburied him at the bottom of the hill, where we

buried all our dead, at nightfall. The man wasn't one of our dead, but we buried him there anyway, because El Tala had become one of our people, and if El Tala was one of our people, then it stood to reason this man should rest in our land.

8

I had been working in Anselmo's market for years. We opened early and closed at sundown, when we opened the bar, which consisted of a few tables we brought outside to drink some gin before we all went home. It had become our custom, in the town, to stop by Anselmo's after a day's work. No one ever missed an opportunity, after returning from the Lopretes' ranch, to tell a story about that cursed world.

We'd been with Tulio the night before, when we got a visit from Fausto. Fausto could work iron better than anyone. Blacksmithing is an art, he always said, his mouth thick with pride. The Lopretes had called him for a job. He was on his way back when he stopped to tell us about this woman, Hermelinda. He said she was the new cook. That she'd come looking for work and been hired right away, to replace old Belma, may she rest in peace. And that there'd been some serious commotion among the ranch hands ever since she arrived. That two men had almost stabbed each other, the other day, on account of this woman: you have to see her, Tulio, she'll take your breath away. She's got all of them out of their minds: the married ones are doing everything they can not to stare and the single ones are strutting around like roosters at a cockfight. She's got these wild eyes and jet-black hair down to her waist. I swear, Tulio, you can't help but want to get lost in that woman until the end of time. Tulio listened closely: I've got to get myself a job on that ranch. Sorry, but the horse has left the stable on that one, said Fausto. Someone's nabbed her already.

9

It was always like that, before a storm. The air curled up quiet against the earth, as if such penance could stave off the lashing to come. We left Anselmo's just in time, each for his own home. The storm started soon after. And it was a big one. As if the sky wanted to tear itself to pieces and rain the debris down on our heads. There was no sleep, from the thunder. It poured all night. Even the next morning, the rain kept its stubborn pace.

We saw him, El Tala, just for a minute as he was leaving. They'd come for him early in the morning, from the Lopretes' ranch: Don Luis had died, he'd been hit by lightning, they needed a coffin. El Tala always had coffins waiting, half-finished, in case of a death. He always told us that you could never make just one coffin: when somebody dies, they always bring someone else with them. That was what he had learned in the rainforest. Out there they say no one dies alone: every death is accompanied by two more, for the journey. So that was why he made his coffins in threes. Now that he had finished one for Ramos, they'd come to ask for one for old Loprete. We would have liked to learn a little more about the man who had come to collapse on Anselmo's doorstep, but El Tala was a man of few words, and ever since that cry of his at Doña Iris's, we were afraid to ask him anything. We didn't want to trouble him. The only thing he'd said to us was how it had been tormenting him, the fact that he hadn't recognized his uncle. He adjusted his hat and kept saying the same thing over and over again: look what they did to him, there was nothing left.

10

The rains, in these parts, aren't to be trusted. They always bring misfortune. El Tala had already left for Loprete's burial when La Colorada appeared in town, screaming her head off. She often went to visit the bottom of the hill on Sundays. She'd bring flowers and stay a while, with her dead. But this time she came back spluttering and gesticulating, eyes wild. Anselmo came out of their house and found her like that. He stood there looking at her, and then managed to get her in a sort of embrace, as if to contain her fear, and he asked her: hey, woman, what happened. But there was nothing to be done. She was out of control, arms flapping up and down, sky to ground, nonsense spewing from her mouth. She didn't seem like the same woman, always so calm, with those eyes like water, now rapt in the throes of her exaltation. Such a stir, we all ended up surrounding her. Her words collided inside her mouth and came out all twisted.

Finally, we understood. We took off for the hill, under that steady drizzle, and found what La Colorada had been trying to tell us: he was gone. The empty coffin lay in the hole. And beside it a pile of earth. Ramos was no longer here among our dead.

11

For a few days we didn't know what to do. El Tala was still away, at the ranch, where he'd been since Loprete's death. We didn't know whether to get the message to him or wait for him to finish his job, whether to cover the hole or just leave it open, because maybe El Tala would want to see it for himself, when he got back. Someone had the idea that we should stand guard at the bottom of the hill: the one thing we knew was that we didn't want anyone to keep running off with our dead. There was already enough commotion with Loprete dying, and now this. No one had ever laid a finger on our land like that before. It was all anyone in town could talk about. From the first rays of dawn, people began whispering about the corpse's disappearance: who would have taken the trouble, why on earth would they do it. The topic occupied every hour of every day, even after the sun had gone and all that remained were stars in the sky.

Finally we decided to ask her, Doña Iris. The two of us went, Anselmo and I. We found her outside, in front of her house, her body hunched over a cooking pot, the fire lit in the middle of the afternoon, moisture still in the air, after the rain. She muttered something, eyes fixed on the pot. She dropped in some herbs and kept muttering.

She hadn't seen us coming. We didn't want to disturb her, so we didn't clap to announce our arrival like we might have on some other day. We had never seen her like that, so absorbed in her cooking pot, nor so absent in her murmuring. It was as if she herself had sunk into the fire. We decided to get a little closer. Then she saw us and made a sign: to give her space, leave her be, wait a while. So that was what we did. We backed up a good ways and stood there in silence, trying not to bother her.

It was already starting to get dark by the time Iris called to us: come. We were so anxious for her help that we just skipped the pleasantries and launched straight into our problem: forgive the intrusion, Doña Iris, but Ramos is gone.

She wasn't surprised, but kept silent, looking at her pot. Then she invited us inside. We walked in cautiously and stayed put, standing. She started bustling around; it seemed like she had a purpose. She went to look for something, and soon came back carrying dried branches, her arms raised, and she shook them, eyes closed, speaking softly, her words disjointed and incoherent. This went on for a while, this back and forth, until she let her arms drop, left the branches on the floor, and looked at us: so you say he's gone. We nodded, silent, and dropped our gazes, careful not to look at her too much, afraid we might distract her from what she had to tell us.

She looked at Anselmo with those penetrating eyes of hers: someone has it out for that man. They're never going to let him rest in peace.

12

When Don Loprete died there was a procession of wagons from the town. Everyone wanted to go, and there were no objections from the Lopretes: the storm, and the death of the old man, had caught them all by surprise. Their only concern was making sure the priest was there. And El Tala, to put the finishing touches on the coffin. They sent word around late afternoon: that everything was ready, that the funeral would be starting soon. Everyone mounted their wagons and set out, as if it were a wedding.

They say everything was more or less going off without a hitch: the priest officiating the service; the five sane brothers in front; the insane wife off to the side, sitting in her chair, accompanied by Iris; the ranch hands and their wives, still in shock; those who had come to offer their condolences to one or another and those who had come from the town, all mumbling their sentiments. They say it was all proceeding in a kind of holy peace, that even the storm seemed to have calmed, as if to ask forgiveness for that night's lightning. But not even the sky's provisional stillness nor the general dismay over the man's sudden death could prevent what happened next: the voice of one of the women tore through the hushed murmurs of the night, crying out that he was a bastard, that she was glad he was dead and he should rot in hell. Those who were nearest to her listened. They turned around, to look at her. Some listened with their eyes glaring, others looked on with pricked ears, and others pointed as if she were a goat that had somehow gotten mixed up in a herd of cows. The sons gave the order to silence her, and some of the ranch hands found themselves having to ask her to go back where she'd come from. I know that woman is my mother, and that Don Loprete was my father, but no one talks about that anymore.

After she was kicked out, a few others followed, and then it didn't take long for the procession of wagons to start back toward the town, under that impenetrable sky of moonless, starless night.

13

Families come together and break apart here like eddies in the wind, as easily as storm clouds in the sky. People talk a lot around here, but don't say much. For years I've been listening to whatever anyone wants to tell me. That I was born on that ranch. That Loprete had his way with my mother wherever, whenever, and as often as he wanted. And that one of those times, she got pregnant and hid it the whole nine months, until she had me. But that she was too young and if she hadn't kept working she would have starved to death. That she handed me over to the Romanos, who had been hoping for a child. And that I lived with them, for a few years, until they died in the fire. Someone carried me out of the fire thinking I was dead too. They say my arms and chest were so burned they didn't know what to do for me. That they healed my body piece by piece, as best they could, until I ended up like this, how I am now: as if someone had stitched together a bunch of scraps of dried leather to cover up what the fire had taken. Some say that I only burned in the front because I had my arms raised, toward the flames, as if the light had come to be my salvation.

Since the fire, Anselmo has acted as my father. His own children had already left home, and he must have still felt that absence. That's how we make families here. With whatever we have at hand.

14

El Tala still wasn't back. We thought they must have given him another big job, something that would take a long time, but we were still uneasy about the business with Ramos. Until then, we had never lost one of our dead. Anselmo wanted to go and break the news: if he doesn't come back tomorrow, I'll go, I'll tell him. I offered to go too. I knew Anselmo was fond of El Tala: he'd treated him like a son ever since El Tala had appeared in town with nothing but the wish to end his journey.

We left early, the next morning, for the Lopretes' ranch. All traces of rain had vanished from the sky; the night's wind had carried off the last clouds. Anselmo started telling me that we were doing the right thing, going to see him, that it wasn't right for everyone else to know but him.

It was still early when we got there. We found the place in complete disarray. Loprete's death had thrown everything into chaos, even the blades of grass in the fields. They were like ants escaped from some stepped-on anthill: all of them out there, running to and fro, stunned and aimless, as if all that activity could lessen the shock. We went straight to the ranch hands' quarters. That was where we found Feliciano: the goatherd who comes down from the quebrada, every summer, to work with the horses. Anselmo always thought highly of him, ever since the time Feliciano helped him rebuild his roof after a storm had tossed it aside like a hat. He was the first one who told us that something was wrong with everyone over there. That they had locked away the four crazy brothers, babbling in the tool shed, while the sane brothers tried to blame each other for the death of their father, who had gone to meet his end on the bridge during that infernal storm, struck by a bolt of lightning. That the crazy brothers had been having an episode that morning, and that that was why their father went to find the doctor. That the widow was rocking back and forth in her rocking chair, raving and lost in her world of demented mutterings, and that although she had been told that her husband was dead, she hadn't seemed to absorb the news at all. And that Doña Iris had been with her a lot, during those days, doing all she could to make her better.

We asked him about El Tala. Feliciano told us that he hadn't seen him since early that morning, but he'd show up soon. And so it was. He showed up at lunchtime, at the ranch hands' quarters. There we were, Anselmo and I, waiting for him. As soon as he caught sight of us he started peppering us with questions, wanting to know if something had happened. Yes, said Anselmo, we came to tell you. And it was like El Tala had ten pairs of ears in his head: we came to tell you that someone took Ramos, right after you left. That was all he needed to hear for his eyes, El Tala's eyes, to darken with rage. We had never seen him like that, with such fury in his eyes. I stayed silent while Anselmo tried to calm him down, but nothing worked. Anselmo gestured to me that we should leave, that we should get him out of here. So that's what we did. And we walked a good while, the three of us, passing by the corrals, while we tried to calm El Tala down and find out, once and for all, where all that wrath had come from. Little by little he got ahold of himself and started to talk. It was the rage that made him open up, I think. El Tala had always been a man of few words. But there's no motivation quite like rage, and he started to talk and didn't stop until he had told us the whole story of Camilo Ramos.

15

Some enmities never die. They take root, deep inside, and grow and grow, little by little, until they explode and release their venom. That was how El Tala spoke, that day, as if filled with a bitterness that was poisoning him from the inside.

He told us how he was thirteen years old when Ramos showed up with the idea of taking him to the rainforest. He said there was work there, with wood. El Tala's parents didn't want to hear anything about it at first, but things were getting bad there, up in the quebrada: it was just too dry. They weren't even getting what little rain they were used to: the rocks themselves were withering for lack of water. Everyone who could was leaving to seek a future somewhere else. So in the end, they let him go. And there really was work out there. They got jobs as soon as they arrived, at the Olayas' sawmill. He told us that the Olayas were very decent when they were new and didn't even have a place to sleep. They made some space for them, in the sawmill, and they were patient, letting them learn on the job. El Tala and Ramos were there for a good long time. Once they were able to rent a room of their own, they found it hard to sleep: they missed the smell of sawdust. Then they got jobs in the workshop, which the Olayas also owned. They made furniture in that workshop. And coffins for burials. That was where El

Tala learned his trade. He seemed to have a gift for it, as if he had been a woodworker in another life and had come into this one still holding on to the memory of his past. But it was harder for his uncle, who had restless hands. One day, a man named Sosa appeared at the workshop. He told them he was a lumber dealer. And that he needed men, for deliveries. He paid well. El Tala's uncle accepted right away, since he'd wanted to move on from the workshop for a while already. El Tala decided to stay: he was treated well, and he liked his work. But it turned out that Sosa didn't so much sell lumber as steal it and then resell it. He and his people. That was how they spent their time. They'd rob people, out on the roads, and make a lot of money. They were infamous, but no one ever said anything. The uncle realized he'd gotten mixed up in some bad business and wanted to get out, but it was too late. One night, when he came back to the boarding house, he was upset. El Tala wanted to know what had happened, but his uncle didn't want to say. In the end, he relented: a job had gone wrong and someone had been badly injured. I'm not going to stay with these people, Tala, we didn't come all this way just to get ourselves into trouble. But the problem was that they wouldn't let him go: don't be a pussy, Ramos, you're just going to have to deal with it, this isn't the kind of thing you can walk away from. That's what they said to him. And Ramos became resentful, after that. He'd spend every day chewing on that resentment, until he got involved with the wrong woman: the one Sosa had his eye on. According to his uncle, it was just a case of bad luck. But El Tala wasn't so sure. He thought his uncle got with that woman as a kind of revenge: he'd had his stomach all tied in knots ever since Sosa refused to let him go. But what happened was Sosa and his men didn't forget the insult. They grabbed him, four of them, one night. After, he dragged himself back to the boarding house, barely able to walk. It was awful to see: lips split, tooth knocked out, his eyes two marbles of black pulp. He was in no condition to go anywhere, but they'd given him a deadline: two hours, and he should be grateful. It was the last time I saw him and I never knew where he went. Before he left, he pulled himself together enough to tell me that there was a place nearby where there was work, that I already knew a trade, that I should go as soon as possible; that he was sorry to say it but my name had come up too while they were giving him that beating. I didn't even get a day.

Two men showed up that very morning and said to me: you'd better leave now or we'll cut off your hands, then we'll see what kind of carpenter you are.

We learned all of this, about El Tala, that afternoon. It didn't seem to have upset him, telling us the story. It was more like he'd just unburdened himself of a fury he'd been bottling up for centuries.

16

We asked him, El Tala, if he was sure that Sosa's men had been the ones who'd stolen Ramos's corpse. His eyes were still blazing when he showed us the scar. It had come from a wound he'd gotten on his hand the day he left the forest. We had always thought he'd hurt himself working with wood. But no. He told us it was those men. They laid their machete into his hand that day, as a warning: that they were sorry but my uncle had fucked with Sosa and no one fucks with Sosa; that I had to get out of there right away and not even think about coming back; that my uncle could run far and wide but it would do him no good; that they'd follow him to the ends of the earth so he would never forget about Sosa; that he would never rest in peace.

17

And there we were, that afternoon, staying with El Tala among the corrals as he shared his memories, unburdening himself, when a woman appeared, her skin all covered in gentle wrinkles, her eyes bright and clear like water, and looked at him, at El Tala, with a sort of miraculous devotion, and we all fell silent, all of a sudden, because the world seemed to stop in its tracks, in that woman's presence. We stood still, as if waiting for something, as the rage abated in El Tala's eyes and an expression of calm settled onto his face: she's my mother, he said, as if that was all that could ever be said. We were astonished as she looked us over, like she was trying to figure out what sort of people we were. This is Anselmo and Rulfino, mother. Don Anselmo was the one who took care of me, this whole time, and Rulfino is like a brother. That was how he introduced us, that afternoon, and then he excused himself: I'll come home, tomorrow, and we'll talk more. He thanked us for the visit and then we saw him walk slowly toward the ranch hands' quarters, next to that woman.

We got up on the wagon, Anselmo and I, and rode awhile in silence. The sun was sinking low in the sky as we went along, neither of us much interested in talking. I guess we were digesting the whole story El Tala had told us. After so many years of seeing him on his own, it was nice to see him walk alongside his mother. Maybe now El Tala would feel like he had a family. Sometimes I like to think that having a family means knowing someone will be waiting for you when you come home.

The wagon was passing over an area of blackened grass when Anselmo extended an invitation: would I like to stay for dinner with them that night.

I accepted.

When we got there, La Colorada was waiting for us, surrounded by the smell of soup, stew, and freshly baked bread.

18

El Tala came home the next day. He arrived late in the afternoon, as we were closing up shop. He'd brought his mother with him: we came to see the pit, he told us. We offered to accompany them. La Colorada gestured to Anselmo: not to worry, she'd take care of the bar. So we left, with El Tala and his mother, to visit the bottom of the hill. They didn't want to go in the wagon or on horseback. On such a pleasant, cloudless afternoon, it would be good to walk. And so that's how we went, walking slowly, to see the pit. We had decided not to fill it until El Tala had a chance to see it. We expected to find the empty coffin at the bottom, just as we had left it, and I had the disturbing thought, as we walked, that this woman was going to find her brother's grave like that, with nothing inside. It made me want to say something, but we were walking single file, the four of us, and there was no opportunity. I stayed silent, carefully watching the expectation on the face of this woman, on her way to see that empty hole in the ground.

The sky was still glowing when we arrived. It was the purple-golden glow of a cloudless summer sunset. The pit was just as we left it, the coffin open, its lid broken, the dirt flattened by the rains we'd had, and everything cast in yellow by the last rays of sun. El Tala was in front, with his mother. We stood a little way back. We didn't want to interrupt them. They hugged, wordlessly, just looking at the hollowed-out ground. Until she sank to her knees and grabbed two fistfuls of dirt to throw to the bottom of the pit, and then more fistfuls, and more fistfuls, one after another and another, as if she could fill the void with a few crumbs of earth. Until she stood and looked at El Tala and hugged him and we heard a slow whimper, coming from them both, at the same time, softly, as if it had just slipped out.

Then we turned back, toward Anselmo's, dragging our feet all the way. El Tala went in front, with his mother. It made my insides churn to see that woman with her head hanging, as if searching for comfort in her own chest, and those little, listless orphan steps, like someone pushing the weight of her grief ahead of her.

As soon as we got into town, El Tala said goodbye: I'm going to take my mother home now, but I'll be back tomorrow, and we'll have plenty of time to talk.

I didn't feel like staying that night. I went home, the long way round, just watching the stars turn in the sky above.

I was just getting to my house when I saw someone there, standing at the door. I didn't recognize her until I got closer: it was the woman who'd given birth to me. I invited her in. I offered her some water. She took a sip, although just a small one, to be polite, and hastened to tell me she'd come to say goodbye. And please would I forgive her: she was so young then. She said that I had been born the day she turned fourteen. That she had sworn to see Loprete to his grave. That now he was dead, she could go. That she was going south, with a friend from the ranch: I want to get as far away as I can from this hateful place. She gave me a rosary. She said it was all she had to give me. That it had been her grand-mother's. Then she excused herself: I have to go, we leave at dawn. I walked her out, and stood watching her shadow as it slipped away, with those deter-mined steps, among the night's trees.

El Tala came back the next day, as he had promised. He was alone, without his mother. Tulio was talking Fausto's ear off at another table. We sat down, me and Anselmo, to talk to El Tala under the pergola.

He told us it was the night of the burial. That was when he'd been reunited with his mother, after the funeral, and that was why he'd stayed over there, with the Lopretes: I offered to help them finish a big project, and they said yes, which was a relief because I didn't want to have to go around explaining how Lina was my mother, how that was the real reason I wanted to stay.

He told us that he had polished the coffin and that they'd filled it with Don Loprete's remains: whatever charred pieces they'd managed to bring down from the high bridge. That when he finished the coffin job he hadn't been sure whether he should stay or go, but then he ran into Feliciano, outside the tool shed, where he'd been polishing the coffin. That they'd gotten to talking and he started to feel like staying awhile. He said a few long tables had been put out with table-cloths and things to eat and drink, and that there were two women, by the tables, coming and going, serving, making sure everyone had what they needed. He said he'd never seen them before, that he didn't remember them at all. Then he realized they worked in the kitchen, in the Lopretes' house. He said he saw Hermelinda first, and that it wasn't hunger that drew him to those tables but Hermelinda's hair, so smooth and so straight. And that he started talking to her until the other woman came over, and when he turned she looked at him so searchingly that he forgot all about Hermelinda: when she looked at me it was like a fire burning, as if I were a saint or a ghost, and then she asked me my name. I'm El Tala, I said, and her gaze bored into me as if she needed to unearth her memories of me before telling me she was my mother. But I didn't need her to tell me: when she'd asked my name, I'd already started looking at her more closely, more deeply, and I saw who she was. She hugged me, and I hugged her back, and there we stayed, the two of us, unwilling to let go.

That was how he told us, El Tala, about reuniting with his mother. But as soon as he finished telling the story, his face fell: there was no denying that Ramos's death was still weighing on him.

We asked if he'd told her, his mother, about all the business with Sosa. No, he said, I don't want to burden her with that too.

21

The air got heavier that afternoon. The heat was crushing, and made us so sluggish that it was all we could do to drag our bones around that day. But it would come soon, the rain. Maybe early the next morning before dawn, or later, once the sun had started to rise. Anselmo wasn't sure whether to open the bar: God knows, we might have a downpour on top of us in no time. I left the shop and went to take the measure of the sky. I came back in and said let's open: there's still a few hours left, before the rain, before it gets here. We started putting out the chairs at seven. Tulio helped us, since he was already outside waiting for his gin. We sat down, the three of us, looking at the shadow cast by the grapevines, praying for a little wind to stir up the quiet heat of the evening.

After a while, Fausto came by. He went up to ask La Colorada for a glass of rum, and then sat down with us. Tulio was talking about Hilaria, the woman who always comes out during the siesta wearing that black wide-brimmed hat of hers, to sit on the bench in the square, every day at the same time, talking to herself as if she had someone beside her. Hilaria became a widow as a result of the fire, the same one that took my parents, the night of the torches. Since then, she goes out dressed in black every afternoon, alone and muttering, to the bench in the square. They say she searched the ashes for her husband for eight long days. And that she slept those eight nights on top of the rubble. That she turned over every piece of charcoal with her bare hands, her back all hunched, one hand first and then the other, repeating the name of her husband, barely stopping to catch her breath: Abel, where are you, Abel. And that was the last thing she said to anyone, because old Lorenza came on the ninth day, to pull her out of it: come on, Hilaria, come, enough sifting through ashes; your husband is dead. Ever since Lorenza took her away, she only comes out in the afternoon, in her black wide-brimmed hat, to talk to herself. Tulio always felt bad for her and watched her. He thought about going and sitting with her, to talk for a while, but he never got up the courage to actually do it. That's what he told us, Tulio, as the sun left its last traces in the sky. The borders of things had already gone blurry when we saw the shadow approaching us. It removed its hat, to greet us: it was Feliciano, who'd taken the day off. Anselmo slapped him on the back a few times; he always liked seeing Feliciano. Anselmo went to get him some rum and we got to talking.

That night we learned that it was Feliciano who'd brought El Tala's mother from the quebrada. He said she was starving when they'd found her, up there, next to the stream. And that he'd been asked to help: to bring her here, so that she could look for work. He'd accepted without knowing that he was bringing El Tala's mother back to him: she's a good woman; ever since she got here she's been trying her best to get used to these parts, but it's been such a shock for her, since all she ever knew were the slow days of the quebrada. She always says to me: back there, the days would just pile up, all the same, one on top of the other, but here there's always something new and important to do and by the time I go to sleep my head's all tangled in knots. Of course the poor woman arrived at an especially strange time, with Loprete's death driving them all out of their minds in that house. I've watched her go from the joy of reuniting with her son to grief over her brother's death, and now the utter bewilderment of finding out his body's been stolen. He finally got up the courage to tell her. There's something in El Tala's voice, something like venom, every time he talks about Sosa and his people. You can feel it, the bad blood he's holding on to, so bitter it would turn your stomach, keep you up at night. Now, we only talk about these things in the quarters, but we all know how that works: a soft tongue pricks the ears. Luis Loprete ended up finding out about Sosa and went straight to find El Tala, wanting to know more: tell me about these men who've come to desecrate our land. So he told him the whole thing from the start. And El Tala got the feeling that this Loprete brother was accusing him of something, like he was saying it was his fault Sosa and his men had come here, to interfere with these lands. El Tala tried to explain: that these were very powerful people, but it was no cause for concern, this wasn't about land. And he told me that as soon as he said it, he saw those eyes, Loprete's son's, turning in their sockets, as if someone had stuck a dagger in his guts. When El Tala saw the way he looked, he could sense the danger and tried to take it all back, but it was too late. Luis Loprete sprang up and looked at him with those venomous eyes: these are our lands.

Someone's going to have to go and tell those people that no one comes here and messes with our graves. I swear on my father's memory: we're going to bring Camilo Ramos back.

22

He didn't look so good, Anselmo, the next morning. He was going around with his head hung low, muttering every now and then. I didn't want to overwhelm him with questions. The rain had come in the early hours, after we'd said goodbye to Feliciano, and it hadn't yet finished pouring its sorrows down on top of us. It raged all morning, until finally its fervor waned, and we were left with an afternoon of meager drizzle and a sky devoid of any conviction other than a refusal to clear.

Anselmo kept muttering. Finally I asked him what was the matter. He told me he was worried about El Tala, that he hadn't liked Feliciano's story one bit: you know what the Lopretes are like. They'll go out like a pack of wild dogs and whatever they bring back will not be good.

He was right: they were always looking for a fight, whenever we saw them ride by on their horses. We knew all too well what happened when they felt insulted. They brought disaster with them wherever they went. Like on the night of the torches, when the Gamboas showed up on their twenty horses, each one with their fire, to settle their scores, and set all our lives ablaze, before dawn.

23

No more than a week had passed since Feliciano let us know that Loprete seemed to have taken offense, when El Tala showed up at Anselmo's. It wasn't hard, from those nervous eyes of his, to tell that he'd come to say goodbye: he was leaving, and that was that. But Anselmo, with his fatherly gaze, refused to understand. Instead, it seemed what he really wanted to hear was that El Tala had come to say that he wasn't going anywhere, that he was staying put, right here, because what was the point of going to settle old scores out there, in the forest. But El Tala stood before us, that afternoon, nodding in acknowledgment with lips pressed tight as if his very soul could escape through his mouth. We were there with Fausto that day: he'd come with Olegario to tell us he and Hermelinda were engaged, and that in June there'd be a party in the town. El Tala didn't sit down or order his gin. We were all standing there when he nodded again, this time to Anselmo: could we go inside for a minute, I want to talk to you about something. We watched them walk away, toward the house. They didn't take long. After a short while they came back out, and I could already see that expression on Anselmo's face. He looked crestfallen as he walked, as if all the bones in his body had just gone slack. El Tala came to us and said, to Tulio and me: forgive me, but

I have to go. We stood to say goodbye. He slapped us each on the back. We returned the gesture.

Anselmo watched him go and then looked at us with eyes of total desolation: he acted like he'd come to ask my permission, but no, the decision had already been made.

24

So El Tala left. He went out the next day, with three Lopretes and four ranch hands. We watched them all head off on their horses. They were going after Sosa and his men, to find those stolen bones. But to me it seemed like this journey to honor the memory of a dead man was going to lead them straight into a nightmare.

The summer was coming to an end. We brought out the tables that evening, and all that remained was a gentle breeze, awaiting the night.

25

By then we didn't have long to wait until the April rains, and this worried me a good deal. Jesús Romano, the father who raised me, had respect for the April rains. And he had his reasons. He always told me that his sister Matilde and every last hair on her head had been carried off by the water one April when the rivers rose. That it had swept her away as if she were a goat, or a cow, on her back, floating belly up, with nothing to grab on to. And that he'd tried to hold on to her but his arms weren't strong enough back then: she slipped from between my fingers. He always told this story and asked us to be careful with water: that it was a wicked thing, that it could carry away your whole life in the blink of an eye, even your story, even your name. That was what he told me: be careful, Rulfino, because water can take away both the living and the dead, jumbling everything together in its rush to get to the sea. And now, every time our April rains are on their way, the nightmares come: coffins floating in that wicked current, all mixed together, wrenched from the earth, bereft of their names. With old Loprete dead now, I can't stand the thought of his coffin getting mixed up with my father's, because they sure could end up confused, in waters like that.

My name is Rulfino Romano and it's not true that I got burned welcoming the light of those flames; I got burned, and I remember it well, because the fire was devouring my father, and I tried to save him.

26

Feliciano came one Sunday, to say goodbye. Every year he left at the end of March. He told us he'd offered to take her, El Tala's mother, back to her part of the world. But that she hadn't wanted to: that she would stay put right here, to wait for her son. That her son had promised to take her to the sea, when he got back.

Anselmo bought him a glass of rum, which turned into several. Feliciano stayed with us a good long while that evening. It was a slow evening, like always when the April rains were close. Evenings of long twilight, resisting their own end, as if they know what's coming but try to keep it at bay as long as they can, in those slow March skies.

27

The rain came the first day of April, like every year. It arrived with the same dogged persistence as always: falling every day from the sky with the same intensity, tirelessly steady, never letting up but never getting worse either. More than rain, it seemed like tears, as if the sky needed to let loose its many sorrows, and it had to rain like that, for so long, until it was empty. We'd gotten used to being covered in mud every April, coming home with our clothes completely soaked, listening to the endless sound of falling water. At first you can smell the scent of wet earth. But as the days stretch on, the scent turns to the stench of dead animals, drowned in their corrals, washed into a corner, trapped in a wire fence. Little by little they start to rot, and the land releases its poisoned breath.

We were already through to the middle of April when the man showed up. He looked like a drunkard, trying to walk through that quagmire. La Colorada was first to notice and told the rest of us that something was moving out there. We were used to finding dying animals there in the flooded land. We went out from the shop thinking it'd be a chicken, or some half-drowned dog. But no. It was a man. He had a donkey with him. We had never seen someone make it to these parts like that before, in the middle of all that water.

28

By May the fields were lakes. Only when the earth could calm its innards and swallow the water that sat atop it could we begin to deal with the death that lay in those fields: orphaned mules, chickens, dogs, the remains of all that dies in April. We'd had a long day, coming and going with the wagon, digging graves, cleaning up the land. We were all on our way back home when the red moon began to emerge, at the far end of town, inching above the horizon. We stopped awhile, to watch. And that was what we were doing when we heard the hoof-beats on the mud-slopped earth. It was still far off, that galloping. Anselmo removed his hat as if to help him see better: what are so many horses doing coming here at this hour, Rulfino?

We stood and waited for them.

The moon had come all the way up by the time they were close enough for us to see their faces. Three Lopretes and four ranch hands. They carried two big sacks.

One held the bones of Camilo Ramos.

The other, El Tala.

WILL MORNINGSTAR is a book editor and translator whose work is featured in Deep Vellum's *Best Literary Translations 2025* anthology and has appeared in journals such as the *New England Review, ANMLY, Two Lines, Latin American Literature Today, Strange Horizons*, and the *Massachusetts Review*, as well as in museums and cultural institutions throughout Spain. He is the publisher of Boston-based Diptych Press, a new initiative to foster dialogue about literature from around the world.

SAMANTHA SCHNEE is the founding editor of *Words Without Borders*, which has published 4,400 writers from 139 countries since the online magazine launched in 2003. As a translator from Spanish, she is the recipient of a 2023 National Endowment of the Arts Literature Fellowship to translate eminent Mexican author Carmen Boullosa's novel *El complot de los románticos* as well as a 2024 Berlin Prize from the American Academy in Berlin to translate Irati Elorrieta's award-winning debut novel, *Luces de invierno*.

Book Club Discussion Guides on our website.

World Editions promotes voices from around the globe by publishing books from many different countries and languages in English translation. Through our work, we aim to enhance dialogue between cultures, foster new connections, and open doors which may otherwise have remained closed.

Also available from World Editions:

Río Muerto
Ricardo Silva Romero
Translated by Victor Meadowcroft
"A wrenching tale of murder and survival in Colombia
by an important Latin American voice."
—*Publishers Weekly*

This World Does Not Belong to Us
Natalia García Freire
Translated by Victor Meadowcroft
"Disquieting and visceral ... García Freire unearths a
brilliant sense of the miraculous from the swarming
and putrid subject matter. The result is beautifully
macabre." —*Publishers Weekly,* *Starred Review*

Abyss
Pilar Quintana
Translated by Lisa Dillman
2023 NATIONAL BOOK AWARD FINALIST
"A triumph of perception and representation."
—National Book Award Judges Citation

The Bitch
Pilar Quintana
Translated by Lisa Dillman
2020 NATIONAL BOOK AWARD FINALIST
"*The Bitch* distills entire social, ethical, and cultural
universes into a potent short novel and offers a
startling, profound portrait of frustrated desire that will
stay with the reader for a long time to come."
—National Book Award Judges Citation

On the Design

As book design is an integral part of the reading experience, we would like to acknowledge the work of those who shaped the form in which the story is housed.

Tessa van der Waals (Netherlands) is responsible for the cover design, cover typography, and art direction of all World Editions books. She works in the internationally renowned tradition of Dutch Design. Her bright and powerful visual aesthetic maintains a harmony between image and typography, and captures the unique atmosphere of each book. She works closely with internationally celebrated photographers, artists, and letter designers. Her work has frequently been awarded prizes for Best Dutch Book Design.

The cover image is a photo taken by Juan Nepomuceno Carlos Pérez Rulfo Vizcaíno, better known as Juan Rulfo. Juan Rulfo was an influential Mexican novelist, photographer, and screenwriter. The image entitled *Nada de esto es un sueño* (None of This Is a Dream), published by Rulfo himself in 1949, has become one of his most reproduced photos, and was also used on the original cover of *Quebrada*. The original photograph is a black-and-white image, which was edited and colored by lithographer Bert van der Horst of BFC Graphics (Netherlands).

The typeface Voga was used for the title. It was designed by Quebec-based designer Charles Daoud, and published in 2014 by his personal foundry, North Type.

Euan Monaghan (United Kingdom) is responsible for the typography and careful interior book design.

The text on the inside covers and the press quotes are set in Circular, designed by Laurenz Brunner (Switzerland) and published by Swiss type foundry Lineto.

All World Editions books are set in the typeface Dolly, specifically designed for book typography. Dolly creates a warm page image perfect for an enjoyable reading experience. This typeface is designed by Underware, a European collective formed by Bas Jacobs (Netherlands), Akiem Helmling (Germany), and Sami Kortemäki (Finland). Underware are also the creators of the World Editions logo, which meets the design requirement that "a strong shape can always be drawn with a toe in the sand."

www.ingramcontent.com/pod-product-compliance
Lightning Source LLC
Chambersburg PA
CBHW032124020726
47494CB00007BA/2224